THE BILLIONAIRE'S MAID

A CHRISTMAS ROMANCE NOVEL (ISLAND OF LOVE SERIES BOOK 3)

MICHELLE LOVE

HOT AND STEAMY ROMANCE

CONTENTS

Made in "The United States" by:

Michelle Love

© Copyright 2020

ISBN: 978-1-64808-712-7

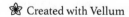 Created with Vellum

BLURB

My hero when I thought I'd lost it all, he wanted more than I could give...
Never had any man attracted me the way he did.
Immediate, primal, carnal in nature—he provoked my inner goddess.
But I had a new job and a new place to live. And he was my boss.
My much older boss, who had much more sexual experience than I.
But—my God—how my body burned for him.
And how eager my heart was to be filled with love for the man.
We were a recipe for disaster: I wasn't in his league, and he didn't believe in love.
And I didn't believe in living a life without it...

CHAPTER 1

Ariel

Although hard, the convertible chair-bed underneath me provided something I'd lacked for quite some time—a place to sleep other than the sidewalk.

"Are you awake, love?" Mother's voice came out scratchy. It had been that way for a while, worsening as time went by. I never thought anything of it as the rasp took over her once clear lilt. I definitely never thought it meant she had throat cancer. But that's exactly what it had meant.

"I am, Mum." I sat up, stretching my sore muscles. "Do you need anything?"

"A shower." She smiled weakly. "And another ten years or so of life."

She liked to joke around about her impending death a bit too much for my taste, but I forced a smile for her. "Don't we all, Mum." I got out of my little bed, which lay right next to her hospital bed. "I'll start the shower then help you get in. No reason to bother the nurse at this hour."

Her pale blue eyes scanned the dimly lit hospital room. "What time is it, Ariel?"

Looking at my watch, I made sure of the time. "Four in the morning."

"Oh, I shouldn't be bothering you for a shower at this hour, love. Go back to sleep." My mother never liked to be a bother.

But I wasn't about to let her go without one single comfort. "No, it's no problem. You've been sleeping so much, I'm sure your internal clock is out of sorts. I'll be right back."

Heading to the toilet, I turned the light on and looked at my reflection in the mirror. Oh, Lord! I look like the walking dead.

After starting the shower, I washed my face in the sink then brushed my teeth. Mother's illness had been rough on me. But then again, life had been rough for us both the last few years.

I'd just turned twenty-one, but my face looked closer to thirty—worn out before my life had even really begun.

My father's death three years earlier had turned our lives upside down. He'd been a little too good at taking care of our every need. Once he and his paycheck were gone, Mum and I had no idea what to do.

The eviction notice came soon after the electricity was shut off. Mum's car was repossessed not long after that. We'd used that as our shelter after we'd gotten kicked out, and without the car, we were left to live on the streets.

Piccadilly Circus in London became our new home. Or more accurately, the shelters and alleys around the square became the places where we laid our heads each night. During the day, we'd walk around picking up loose change and doing anything we could to make a few pounds.

As horrible as it sounds, Mum's passing out in one of the shops had put a roof over our heads, food in our tummies, and a bed under our sore bodies. The hospital took care of us both. But once Mum passed on—and I knew it wouldn't be long now—I would no longer have a place to stay.

Feeling that the water had warmed enough, I went to get my

mother. "Your shower is ready." I helped her out of bed, carefully holding her close to my side to help her walk the few feet it took to get from the bed to the toilet. The ever-present IV made things a little hard, but I'd learned to manage the bulky stand and the line that ran into my mother's chest. The PICC line was a necessity if she wanted to be pain-free most of the time.

As far as treatment for her cancer was concerned, the doctors had recently run out of options. The day prior, the doctor had decided to stop both the radiation and the chemotherapy treatments as they weren't working to reduce the mass in her throat.

"Ariel, I'm feeling a little odd." Mum tried to clear her throat. "It feels like it's getting bigger."

My heart ached for her. "Try not to pay any attention to it, Mum. Focus on anything other than that lump in your throat."

"It's a bit difficult." She ran her hand over her throat. It had swollen to a size I couldn't believe—and in such a short time.

"Just try, Mum." I picked up the detachable shower head to wash her hair. What was left of it, anyway. "Maybe your hair will come back now that they've stopped the chemo."

"Do you really think so?" She smiled a little. "Wouldn't that be nice?" She grasped my wrist suddenly, and I looked at her. "Ariel, I don't want to be buried the way your father was. Please don't let them do that to me. I want to be cremated. My ashes can be spread over his grave. Promise me that's how you'll take care of it."

I hated when she spoke this way, but I knew it was important to her. "I promise you I will do whatever you want, Mum."

"Thank you." She closed her eyes as I finished washing her hair then took the sponge and washed the rest of her thin and frail body. "You're a very good daughter, love. But you must start thinking about what you'll do when the time comes. You can't live in this hospital. You need to see about getting a job. I don't want you living on the streets alone. It's much too dangerous. Even with me there to protect you, things happened that I wish wouldn't have."

"I know." I had no idea what I would do for a job. I had an eleventh grade education and didn't know what marketable skills I could possibly have. When my father died, I quit going to school to take care of my mother. Even before she got sick, she'd always been frail, and she was a mess without my father. She didn't know what to do with herself, and she cried all the time. I couldn't leave her alone.

With the shower done, I turned the water off then wrapped her in a towel. "I'll go grab a fresh hospital gown for you." Leaving her sitting on the small chair in the walk-in shower, I hurried, not wanting to leave her too long. She couldn't handle a fall in her present state.

The sound of her coughing sped me up even more. When I came back with the gown in hand, she was gasping for breath as the coughing fit kept going on and on.

I turned the shower back on, directing the hot water away from her. Steam soon filled the air, and the coughing began to ease up. Shaking, her eyes full of fear, she clung to my arm. She didn't have to say a word. I could read it in her eyes: death was getting closer by the minute.

All dressed and safely back in bed, my mother went right to sleep. The whole ordeal had worn her out. I climbed back into my chair-bed, but sleep evaded me.

What am I going to do?

I was so tired of asking myself that same question over and over again. A few answers would spring up in my brain, but none that I could get to work on right then. I had to be there for Mum. I couldn't take any time away from her to find a job, much less do a job.

Things were at a standstill for me. Waiting for the inevitable to happen, there was nothing else I could do other than be there for my mother.

I must've fallen asleep, as I felt a hand on my shoulder some time later, gently shaking me awake. "Miss Pendragon?"

Opening my eyes, I saw a blur of white, then rubbed the sleep from my eyes to see Mum's doctor standing over me. "Doctor Ferguson?"

"Yes, it's me." He walked to the other side of the small room, heading for the door. "Can you come outside to talk to me?"

Getting up, I tried to smooth out my dress then ran my hand through my hair to tame it a bit. "Yes, sir." I knew I looked like death warmed over, but I followed him out the door anyway.

Just on the other side of the door, the older man looked me over. "Miss Pendragon, I've been worried about you. My wife and I have been discussing your situation."

"You have?" I was surprised. I had no idea he'd been thinking about me at all, much less that he cared about me.

"We have." Pulling his black-rimmed glasses off his face, he reached into the pocket of his white coat and then handed me a piece of paper. "This is the number of a man who I think can help you. I called him last night to tell him about you. He thinks he can find a position for you at his resort. He owns an island in the Caribbean, and he has visitors from all over the world. His guests are typically wealthy people who are there to be catered to and demand privacy while they're there."

"And you think he'll give me a job?" I asked as I looked at the number on the paper. A name—Galen Dunn—was written just above it. "Galen Dunne? Why does that name sound familiar?"

"He's an extremely wealthy Irishman, and he's gained some fame for his inventions and investments." The doctor pulled his cell out of his pocket then showed me a news report with the man's picture on it. "This is him, here."

Blue eyes that seemed to look directly at me even from a mere picture shone from the screen. Dark waves hung to his broad shoulders. The suit he wore looked expensive and seemed to have been made just for him. His muscles were easily noticeable underneath the dark fabric.

"You said you've already spoken to this man?" I wasn't sure what a man like that would expect from an employee.

"I have." The doctor looked down the hallway as some beeping took his attention. "Look, I've got to go. They'll be moving your mother to hospice care today. That means you'll no longer be able to stay with her. You'll be on your own, Miss Pendragon. Mr. Dunne has promised me he'll take care of things for you—give you a job and a place to live. He'll even get you to his island. But you've got to make the call and reach out to him yourself. He's just that kind of man. He likes helping people, but first he wants to see that they're ready to help themselves."

With a nod, I asked, "Can I use the phone in Mum's room to make the call?"

The doctor sighed then handed me his cell. "No. This is a long distance call, and the hospital won't pay for that. Use my cell while I go check on my patient."

Taking his phone, I dialed the number, crossing my fingers that I would say the right things to the only person who could help me.

After a few rings, a woman picked up. "Galen Dunne's office. How can I help you?"

I froze, unable to speak.

"Hello? Anyone there?"

I heard a man's voice in the background, "Nova, who is it?"

"I'm not sure. Maybe the connection is bad. I can't hear anything," she told him.

"Here, give me the phone," the man said. "Galen Dunne here. What can I do for ya?"

His deep Irish voice was so smooth, so commanding. My mouth opened, and words finally spilled out. "I'm Ariel Pendragon, sir. Doctor Ferguson told me to call you. He said he spoke to you about me?"

"Ah, Ariel Pendragon from London," his tone bore a certain amount of concern. "And how is your mother, my dear?"

"Well, she's not going to get any better, sir." I clenched my fist at my side, still angry at the unfairness of it all. "They're sending her to another ward today. Hospice, whatever that is. The doctor said I couldn't go with her."

"He also told me that you and your mother were homeless." He hesitated before going on, "Is that true?"

"Yes, sir, it's true. I don't know where I'll be going once they move my mum." Tears began to burn the backs of my eyes. "The doctor said that you might give me a job at your resort. I would take anything, sir. No job is beneath me."

"Do you have any experience at all?" he asked.

"No, sir, I don't have any experience. I dropped out of school in Year 12 and have been taking care of Mum ever since. That's all I have, sir." It felt humiliating having to tell him that.

"Not to worry, my dear," he sounded so nice. "I can help you. You do want to improve your situation, don't you?"

"I do want to better myself. I will do anything, sir—anything you want me to." I thought better about what I'd said and specified, "Besides doing you any physical favors, sir. I hope you understand what I'm saying?" I felt myself blush, but I wanted him to know that there were some things I wasn't willing to do—no matter how desperate I was.

He laughed. "My dear, I'm not in the habit of having to pay for a woman's company. Not to worry, I'm thinking more along the lines of a maid. I'm in need of a personal maid here at the resort. My old maid has moved on; she met someone and has recently left my employment. So, when can you start?"

"As soon as you can get me there." I could barely breathe. "My mother will be so relieved, sir. Thank you so very much."

"I'll charter a jet to bring you to Aruba right away. From there, my yacht will pick you up and bring you to the island." He'd made everything so easy. "And don't worry about trying to find clothing and anything else to bring with you. I understand what it means to be homeless. You'll be provided with all the clothing, shoes, and toiletries you'll need. I'll set up a bank account for you once you get here. Give me your number, dear."

"I don't have a cell phone, sir." I prayed that wouldn't be a deal-breaker for what he was offering me.

"I'll have Jeffrey give you one. Text me from at this number once you get it, so I'll have your number." He'd fixed my problem so quickly.

"Thank you, Mr. Dunne. But who is Jeffery?" I asked, not having a clue who he was talking about.

"Doctor Ferguson," he clarified for me. "I'll send you a text when you can get to the airport. See you soon, Miss Pendragon."

"Yes, sir. Thank you so much—I won't let you down. Goodbye." I ended the call, then went to find the doctor to give him his phone.

I couldn't wait to tell Mum the fantastic news!

CHAPTER 2

Galen

The girl had sounded so frail over the phone that morning. My heart ached for the poor thing, and I'd known right away I had to help her.

Jeffery and I had become friends while working together on a medical project some years back. When he called to ask me if I had some kind of a job for a poor, homeless young woman—who was also about to lose the only parent she had left—I'd felt my heart breaking for the stranger.

As I sat in the office, my personal cell rang, and I saw it was Jeffery calling. "Hello, Jeffery. I asked you to give me a call because I've got a favor to ask you."

"Ask away, my friend," he said, sounding chipper.

"I need you to purchase Miss Pendragon a cell phone. It can be one of those throwaway, pay-as-you-go things. She'll only need it until she arrives here. I don't want her without a means of communication while traveling." I thought about all the terrible things that could happen to the young woman and didn't want any other misfortunes to happen to the poor creature.

Jeffery was very helpful. "I'll get her one in the gift shop here at the hospital. She's in the room with her mother right now. Her mother was overjoyed when Ariel told her the news. Mrs. Pendragon is very thankful for you, Galen. She's gone on at least a hundred times since Ariel gave her the great news that you're a true blessing to her and her daughter."

Although happy they were so appreciative, I felt saddened by their situation. "I'm the one who's blessed to even be able to help them. Tell me, Jeffery, do you think Ariel will be okay, leaving her mother behind?" I'd been thinking about that a lot since we'd talked. "I don't need her to leave her mother to come to me so quickly. I don't want to take any time away from what she has left with her mother."

"To be honest, leaving now might be best for Ariel and her mother," he told me. "Her mother is about to be taken to hospice, and she'll only get worse from that point on. It's not a process that's appealing, and her daughter will have better memories of her mother if she leaves now. And sometimes it's easier for people who are that sick to pass on if they're not worried about holding on for their loved ones. I've already spoken to them both, and Mrs. Pendragon has told me what she wants done after she dies. I've promised Ariel that I'll personally take care of fulfilling her mother's wishes to be cremated and for her ashes to be spread over her husband's grave."

"That's very kind of you, Jeffery." I thought his actions bode well for both the mother's and daughter's integrity. "I would guess these two women have affected you because they have pure hearts. It's a shame what's happened to them."

He sighed. "They're as kind as they come, Galen. They've told me how things got so bad for them. Mrs. Pendragon got married when she was very young—right out of high school—and her husband pampered his girls a bit too much. He never let them raise a finger to help when it came to meeting the bills, nor did he allow his wife to even purchase groceries. She never had a bank account, never even learned to drive until they had their only child. Only then did Mrs. Pendragon learn so she could take Ariel to school."

"It sounds like he truly loved them, but he did his family a disservice by not encouraging their independence." I found it a bit archaic in this day and age, but guessed it still happened from time to time.

Jeffery agreed, "Yes, he loved them, but failed to teach them much about how to get on in life. Ariel seems sharp enough. I think she can learn. Hopefully, she'll take the opportunity you're giving her and run with it—make a real life for herself. I hope you can get someone to teach her the basics like how to pay bills, to budget, and things like that."

"I'll make sure she gets the help she needs." I'd never before felt such sympathy for a person without even knowing them. "Once you give her the cell, remind her to text me. Since you think it best for her to leave her mother and she seems to agree, I'll charter a private jet now. How long do you think she needs before leaving?"

"Give her a few more hours. Her mother will be settled in by then, and she won't have a place to stay anyway." He laughed. "You know, they both were the happiest I've ever seen them with this news. This is a huge relief to Mrs. Pendragon. I can see she feels at peace now. You really are doing a heroic deed, Galen."

"Well, you're the one who thought of it." I thought that made him a hero, too. "I guess that's why we're such good friends. Great men think alike."

"I suppose so." I heard some odd beeping in the background. "Got to go. I'll get her the cell as soon as I have a moment to do so. Bye now."

I ended the call then looked at my resort manager, who had been listening to my end of the call the entire time. "So, we've got a new girl coming, Nova. Can I count on you to get everything she'll need and get it over to staff housing?"

Nova tapped a pencil on her desktop. "When she texts you, can you ask her for her clothing and shoe sizes? And this might seem a little forward, but you did say the girl is homeless, so ask her for bra and panty sizes, too."

Running my hand over my face, I nodded. "I could do that. Or better yet, I'll just give you her number, and you can text her those questions. I don't want her to think I'm some kind of a pervert."

"You're right." Nova laughed. "I can get the room ready for now. The flight to Aruba from London is about thirteen hours, right? I guess she'll be here sometime tomorrow. I've got plenty of time to get everything she'll need."

I wanted Ariel Pendragon to have more than just the basics. "I want you to go to the boutiques here on the island and get her some nice things to wear. Throw in some jewelry and perfumes, too, why don't you? I want her to feel like she's special. I'm sure sleeping on the streets of London for the last few years has made her feel anything but that."

Nova smiled at me. "What a big heart you have, Galen. I had no idea." She blushed. "I mean, not that you're a tyrant or anything like that. I just mean that I've never seen this side of you is all."

"To be perfectly honest, I've never been in this position before, so I've never really seen this side of me, either." It might be new territory, but it felt right—natural, even. "When I got the call from Jeffery last night, it did something to me. I dreamt all night long about this poor girl and her mother, imagining them out on the streets for years. It made me sick, quite frankly. Thinking that humanity could allow something like that to happen to innocent people...it did something to my heart. All I know is that I'm going to change that young woman's life for the better, and that's that."

"How honorable of you, Galen." Nova got up to leave her office. "I'm going over to staff housing. I want to take care of this myself. Your feelings about this must be contagious, and I want to make sure she get more than the bare minimum. Let's give her a real welcome to our little slice of paradise, shall we?"

I loved Nova's spirit. "I'm glad you took this job. Camilla was my right hand at this resort, and I wasn't sure how her leaving would affect the place. But she's trained you so well, and you've got such a natural gift for caring for others that you've only enhanced our world."

She looked at me over her shoulder just before leaving the office. "Thanks, boss. It's always nice to know I'm making a difference."

From the very first moment I started thinking about opening the resort, I knew I wanted to create the kind of work environment that not only worked to serve others, but also made the employees feel at home. I was so pleased that I'd been able to make that vision a reality, and now we would add another person to our little island paradise. I just prayed that she would find peace here, the way all of us had. It would be my personal mission to help her find it.

I couldn't imagine not having any family to turn to—that sounded so terrible to me. I had such a big, loving family and had no idea what it would feel like to be alone in the world, nor did I want to know how that felt.

When a text came in, I looked at the number and saved it to my contacts under Ariel Pendragon. Then I sent the number to Nova before calling the girl once more. "Hello?" Ariel answered.

"It's nice to hear your voice, Miss Pendragon. I just wanted to let you know that I've set up the jet at Heathrow airport. You can go whenever you're ready. There's absolutely no rush at all." I didn't want her to feel compelled to leave her mother before she had to.

She sniffled a little. "They just took my mother from the hospital. She and I have said our goodbyes, sir. I'll leave for the airport now. Everyone I had here is gone or will be gone soon, so I don't have a reason to stay in London any longer. Doctor Ferguson has assured me that my mother will be kept out of pain and kept comfortable. I thank you for this opportunity to move on with my life, Mr. Dunne. It has been such a help not only to me, but to my mum, too. Now she can move on in peace, not having to worry about what will happen to me."

The way my throat was closing up surprised me. Emotion nearly took me over as I felt the backs of my eyes burning. "This will be your home now, Miss Pendragon. Safe travels, my dear girl. Check in with me when you get on the plane, please. I want to know where you are and that you're safe."

"Thank you. I'll keep you informed, sir. And please, call me Ariel.

Goodbye," her voice cracked as she said the last word. I knew she'd broken down then.

Putting the phone down on the desk, I put my face in my hands as I allowed the sorrow to take me over. Giving in to such emotions wasn't like me, but it seemed I'd already formed a connection with the young Ariel Pendragon.

CHAPTER 3

Ariel

Although my heart ached for my mother, I did find solace in the fact that I finally had a direction for my future. I'd never even been on a commercial airplane before, yet there I was, sitting on a private jet. Such luxury was completely foreign to me, but I could see that would change.

I'd been able to sleep peacefully in the comfortable bed at the back of the plane. After I woke up, I took a shower, fixed my hair, and even did my makeup with the toiletries that were stocked in the lavatory.

The attendant had shown me around the jet when I first arrived. There had been a change of clothing all the way down to a bra, panties, and a pair of sandals in the closet. I'd given my sizes to Nova, the manager of Paradise Resort, only an hour before arriving at the airport. The idea that they'd managed to purchase all that for me in such a short time made my head spin.

Nova had also assured me that there would be plenty of clothing for me and everything else I'd need waiting for me on the island. She even sent me pictures of the bedroom suite I would be staying in.

My new reality was so much better than any dream I could've ever thought up on my own. And I had Doctor Ferguson and Mr. Dunne to thank for that. They were my real-life angels. I would never forget what they'd done for me.

Being able to leave my mother with the knowledge that I would be better than okay was a gift I'd never expected to get. My life was changing for the better, and I couldn't have been more excited for what was to come.

But at the same time, I was losing my mother, and I couldn't have been sadder. The mix of emotion proved hard to take. I was feeling a bit crazed, trying to manage so many extreme feelings.

When the pilot came on the speaker, I jerked my head off the soft pillow. "We're about to land in Aruba, Miss Pendragon. Can you please get to your seat and buckle up?"

Getting up off the bed, I gave myself one last look in the mirror before landing. The reflection staring back at me looked quite different from how I'd looked the last few years. The fancy soaps, shampoos, and conditioners I'd found had made a major improvement.

Heading into the cabin, I took a seat then buckled up. The attendant came out to check on me. "Did you have a nice nap?"

"I had a wonderful nap, thank you." I picked up the bottle of water I'd left in the cup holder by the seat before I'd gone to lie down. "So, we're about to arrive. Is it weird that my stomach feels like something is jumping around in it?" I took a long drink to quench my thirst.

She smiled at me. "I think mine would, too, if I were in your situation. You're about to embark on quite a journey."

A journey?

Yeah, I guess it could be called that. "My whole life is about to change. I hope I do well with it."

"I hope you do, too." She took a seat across from me and buckled her seatbelt. "I've heard a lot about Galen Dunne, but I've never met him. He's quite the handsome man from what I've seen. I think I read last year that he was still a confirmed bachelor and about to turn forty. He sure doesn't look that old, does he?"

I had only seen the one picture of him, but I had to agree. "No, he certainly doesn't look old at all." If he'd been turning forty a year ago, that meant he was most likely forty-one—twenty years older than me. Not that it mattered. He would be my boss, nothing more than that. "He's been very pleasant every time we've talked. I think it'll be nice to work for him."

"I bet it will be," she agreed. "I've only heard good things about him."

The plane began its descent, and I clutched the armrests as I closed my eyes. "Almost there," I whispered to myself.

Once the plane touched the ground, I opened my eyes and laughed. The attendant laughed as well. "We made it."

Nodding, I couldn't get the smile to leave my face. "So, I've got a boat to catch, and then I'll be at my new home. This is so surreal."

"It is, isn't it?" She unbuckled her seatbelt as the plane came to a stop. "Ready to begin your adventure?"

"More than ready." My tummy was twisting and turning, but I wouldn't let that hold me back. "I hope my nerves go away soon. I hate feeling this way."

"You should call Mr. Dunne to let him know you're here," she told me as she got up. "I'll open the door so that you can get on your way."

Pulling out my new cell, I turned it on then made the call. "Ariel?" he answered.

"Yes, sir, it's me. I've just landed in Aruba. What should I do next?" I followed the attendant out the jet's door and walked down the stairs that had been pushed up to the aircraft.

"You should just stop right there. I'm coming out to the tarmac to get you." The sun was so bright I had to shield my eyes as I looked around for him. Then I felt a hand on my shoulder as someone came up behind me. "Hey there."

Turning around, I saw the man face-to-face for the first time. The man was such an eyeful that my words almost stopped in my throat.

"Mr. Dunne, it's so good to meet you. I certainly didn't expect you to come out here to get me. What a pleasant surprise."

"Well, I didn't want you to have to worry about how to get around." He took my hand then placed it in the crook of his arm. "This way. I've got a car waiting to take us to my yacht." He looked at me for a moment, then pulled something out of the pocket of his shorts. "Here, you can have these. They're a necessity here."

I took the sunglasses he'd handed me then put them on. "Thank you, sir. How considerate of you."

"Ah, that English accent of yours is going to be nice to hear." The smile he wore couldn't have been faked. "I'm so glad you're here, Ariel."

"Me, too." I peeked at him out of the side of my eyes, knowing my curiosity would be hidden by the dark glasses: he stood a foot taller than me; his body was even more muscular than it appeared to be in the picture I'd seen of him; he smelled like sunshine and sea breezes; his hair moved in dark waves over his broad shoulders as the wind whipped it around his gorgeous face. I'd never been around such a handsome man before. It felt weird, but a fantastic kind of weird.

Getting into the back of a small car, I felt a bit awkward as Mr. Dunne slid in next to me. The car was so small that our legs touched. "They don't have anything larger than this here. Sorry about that, Ariel," he apologized.

"It's fine." I looked out the window as the driver sped off. "This place is pretty. So different from London."

"I hope you learn to love it the way I do." He put his arm across the back of the seat. "I hope you don't mind me doing this. I've got to stretch out a bit. This car is so cramped, and I've never liked small spaces."

His knees were nearly up to his chin, so I knew he wasn't just throwing out a line. "No, that's fine."

"I don't wish to stir up any bad feelings, but I must ask how you're handling this whole thing," he said with a sympathetic tone to his deep voice. "I don't want you to hesitate to tell me how you're feeling about your mother and what she's going through. And the job, too. I want you to feel free to talk to me about anything. Your situation would be difficult for anyone, Ariel. I don't want you to feel alone."

"Um, thanks." I didn't know what to say. "At this moment, I'm a bit overwhelmed."

"I suppose I would be, too, if I were in your shoes." The way he smiled made me feel safe—a feeling that had become rare in the last few years of my life. "Once the overwhelmed feeling goes away, feel free to talk to me."

"Yes, sir." I ran my hand over the yellow dress. "And thank you for the dress and shoes and stuff." I didn't want to mention the under-clothing to him. "I didn't expect this, but it certainly was welcomed. I looked a fright before I had a shower and got to use all the fancy things in the lavatory."

He took a chunk of my hair between his finger and thumb. "These auburn curls must've proven hard to tame while living on the streets. I'm glad you were able to give them a proper shampooing."

The way his wrist rested on my shoulder as he toyed with my hair stirred odd sensations in my nether regions. That wasn't a good sign. The man was my boss. And he could never be anything more than that.

I had a job and a home now; I couldn't mess that up by having an attraction to the man who'd given me everything. The only thing I could do was ignore the growing moisture that had begun to accumu-late in my new panties. Panties he'd purchased for me.

Oh, hell, girl, you've got to stop.

"Here we are. We're at the dock where my yacht awaits." The car stopped, and Mr. Dunne got out, reaching in to take my hand. "Come now, give me your hand, Ariel. I can't wait to show you my pride and joy. Lady Killer is the latest yacht I've added to my collec-tion. It's got it all. A hot tub, a steam room, an ice machine. And the cook has made us a fabulous lunch. I hope you enjoy fresh seafood."

"I've never had it." He didn't let go of my hand as he led me to his boat. "Not fresh, anyway, only frozen."

"Oh, I didn't think about that." He pulled me up to walk by his side, still holding my hand. "Well, I should think you'll like it. My chef could make a twig taste delicious. He's a genius."

"I'm sure I'll love everything." I couldn't stop looking at all the grand boats that lined the dock we walked down. Then we stopped in front of the 'Lady Killer,' its name proudly painted on the back end of the yacht. "Oh, my! This is gorgeous, Mr. Dunne."

"Thank you! I quite agree with you, Ariel." He took a step onto the deck of the yacht. "Come aboard, my dear. Your new life begins now."

And what a life it should be!

4
___

CHAPTER 4

Galen

I'd begun chatting away in a manner quite unlike my usual self. The woman—the much younger woman—had a way of making me slightly nervous for some reason. I'd yet to release her hand, so I let it go. "Sorry about that. I didn't mean to hold onto you for so long."

She blushed as she took a seat inside the yacht's cabin. "No reason to apologize, sir."

Taking a seat across from her, I resolved to keep a certain amount of distance between us. Ariel hadn't even cleaned all the way up yet, and already I found her extremely attractive—a thing I shouldn't have even been thinking about. The poor woman wasn't emotionally available, what with her mother's illness and impending death weighing so heavily on her mind. Not to mention that I was her employer.

No, any thoughts of Ariel's physical attributes should be shoved far, far away.

Trying to say something comforting, I asked, "You did give the hospice your cell number, didn't you?"

"I did, sir," she answered with a nod. They've promised to call me." She stopped then looked away. The back of her hand ran across her cheek, wiping away a lone tear. "When she passes."

God, I'm an idiot!

Hopping up off my seat, I moved to sit next to her, putting my arm around her narrow shoulders. "I'm so sorry. I don't know why I can't seem to say the right thing, Ariel. Of course, you don't wish to talk about this right now. I'll stop talking about anything that has to do with what you're going through."

Shaking her head, she sniffled. "No, no. I'm the one who's sorry, sir. You've given me this wonderful opportunity, and I've let my emotions overrule me. I need to toughen up and stop taking the things people say to heart."

She was so wrong. "Ariel, until things get better for you, I want you to be my guest at the resort, not an employee. You'll not be doing any work until you've had time to mourn your mother and grieve properly."

Pulling the sunglasses off, she looked right into my eyes. I'd never seen eyes like hers before—the deepest shade of green. "Sir, please allow me to get right to work. It will do me good. Sitting alone and drowning in my grief...that sounds horrifying. I want something that will take my mind away from my mother. I know that might sound shallow or make me sound like a bad daughter, but I need to work. I've never had the opportunity to work before, never had the opportunity to learn a job. I feel this is my time to start growing into the person I'm meant to be. But I am deeply moved by your offer, sir. Very deeply moved."

The softness of her voice soothed me in a way I'd never experienced. The awkwardness I'd felt at making her cry all but left me. "Okay. Whatever you feel is best, Ariel. Only know that I want you to be happy here. I want this experience to enrich your life in a way you'd never imagined it could."

"It has already turned into something I couldn't have even dreamed of, sir, and that's all because of you and Doctor Ferguson. You two are like my guardian angels." She shook her head and laughed a little as though she thought her words were far-fetched. "I suppose my father had a hand in this. I kept thinking that he was watching over us from above, trying to make things better for me and Mum. Maybe he just wanted her with him so badly, and that's why she became ill. And maybe he wanted me to have a better life—one I could never have had back in London. Whatever it is, I'm just thankful to have you."

I traced one finger along her jawline. Despite my earlier resolve to keep things professional, I felt captivated by her words. I couldn't help myself. "I'm thankful to have you, too, Ariel Pendragon," I whispered, gazing into those emerald pools.

Her pink lips pulled up to one side and the corners of her eyes crinkled a tiny bit. "That is nice to know. I think I'll be extremely happy here."

"I hope so." My finger left her face as my eyes went to the chef's assistant, who approached with shrimp cocktails. "Hello, Paolo. This is Ariel Pendragon. She'll be working on the island."

After placing the platter on the coffee table, he extended his hand to Ariel, who took it with a quiet greeting.

"So nice to meet you, Ariel." He was close in age to her, I couldn't help but notice. "Your accent is British, is it not?" He gave her a charming smile, a dimple appearing in one cheek.

"I'm from London." She smiled back at him, and my chest swelled a bit with what felt a lot like jealousy—an emotion I didn't think I was capable of feeling. "And you sound Spanish."

"Because I am from Spain." He laughed, then winked at her. "I live in staff housing, as will you. I'll show you all around the island once you get settled in, Ariel. If you have any questions, feel free to come to me. But I think you will be fine; everyone is very nice. We don't have any drama on our island."

I leaned over to pick up a shrimp, dunking it into the cocktail sauce. "She's having a bit of an upset right now, Paolo. I think we should allow Ariel to join social groups when she feels ready to. I don't want her forced into anything." I looked at the young man. "You understand me, don't you?"

He looked at Ariel, his brown eyes drooping. "I'm sorry to hear you're having a tough time. When you're ready, don't hesitate to tell me so."

"My mother is dying from throat cancer." Ariel shifted a little in her seat, her hand brushing the top of my thigh, which set off an immediate physical reaction. My cock went into a semi-hardened state that I hoped neither of them took notice of. What bad form, getting a semi while the girl discussed her mother's impending death. "Mr. Dunne was contacted by my mother's doctor, and he offered me a job here. I hope I'll be able to settle in quickly and start my new life. When I feel ready, I will join you, Paolo. Thank you so much for your hospitality. It's welcomed."

Paolo's face went pale as he realized the extent of her upset. "Oh, I had no idea. Not to worry, I will not be telling anyone else about your terrible circumstances. And if you ever need a friend or someone to talk to, please feel free to come to me."

"It's okay if you talk to people about me, Paolo," she said. "I'm not hiding anything. It's fine if you find yourself being asked questions; it's only natural that people would be asking who I am."

I could see the young man was a bit shaken by Ariel's story, as he nodded and then walked away. Just then I noticed that I was once again nearly on top of the young woman, our bodies having somehow drifted closer together at some point.

Picking up the crystal cup with the shrimp cocktail I'd already dug into, I got up and went to sit on the seat across from her again. "I suppose my concern for you has me doing things that are a little odd for a couple of people who've just met. Sorry about that, Ariel."

Leaning up, she picked up the other cup then sat back. "Please don't be concerned about me, sir. People have to deal with things like this every day. I'm not special."

"I reckon it's about time you do feel special, Ariel." Looking off to one side, I tried to find the right words. "You're life hasn't been ordinary—not everyone is left to live on the streets. Not everyone loses their father, then their home and all of their possessions. Not everyone loses their mother so soon after all of that. And you are special. A lot of other young women in a similar situation have turned to crime, drugs, alcohol, even prostitution. You didn't do any of those things. Do you know why I think that is, Ariel?"

Shrugging, she whispered, "Because I'm special?"

"Precisely." I ate another shrimp and tried to lighten things up. "With your rare beauty, I imagine you were subject to a lot of propositions from slimy men. Am I right?"

She nodded. "My mother would run them off, threatening them with beatings that would put them within an inch of their immoral lives."

"Had she not been there, would you have fended them off yourself?" I asked, curious.

"It's not in me to sell my body, sir. That's exactly why I told you that over the phone before I came here." She popped a shrimp into her mouth then closed her eyes as she chewed it.

I could tell she liked it. "Tastes fresh, doesn't it?"

She nodded. "So yummy."

Lorena, the bartender I'd brought along for the trip, came up from below with a pitcher of our signature cocktail sitting on a tray alongside a couple of highball glasses.

"Hello! I've made up something special to welcome you to your new work family and home, Ariel. Paolo has filled me in a little on your story, and I just wanted to say hello and offer my condolences about your mother. I'm Lorena, and I work at the various bars on the resort. And I wanted to offer my friendship to you, too. When you're ready, of course." She placed the tray on the coffee table between Ariel and I, then looked at me. "Is this okay for you, Mr. Dunne? Or would you rather I bring you a nice Scotch?"

"This is fine, Lorena." I looked at Ariel. "Paradise Blues is the resort's signature cocktail. It's very refreshing. Taste it. Let me know what you think."

She eyed the blue liquid with curiosity. "How much alcohol is in it?"

Lorena poured some of the drink over a glass filled with ice. "It's mild. One drink won't impact you much. It's certainly not enough to get you drunk."

"I've never had alcohol." Ariel took the glass Lorena offered her. "It looks delicious."

"It is," Lorena gushed. "It's got freshly squeezed fruit juices and coconut water, and the only liquor is coconut rum. It has a low grade of alcohol. Don't chug it—sip it and you'll be fine."

Ariel put the glass to her pink lips, then took a sip. "Oh, Lord, this is the most delicious drink I've ever had." Ariel laughed as she looked at me. "I'm already trying new things—things I never would've known about if I hadn't met you, Mr. Dunne. Thank you so much. You really have no idea how much I appreciate everything you've done for me."

Her smile was infectious, and I found one plastered on my face, too. "I've got so much I'd like to introduce you to, young lady. You're about to see the finest things in the entire world, my dear. I never want you to think that I brought you here—to my island paradise— just to keep you here. I see great potential in you, Ariel, and I want to help you explore it. You will travel the world with me. See things you might've only seen in pictures. Showing you things you never would've had the chance to see in your old life will be my greatest pleasure."

Lorena's dark eyes went wide as she looked at Ariel. "Damn, girl. You've struck gold here with Mr. Dunne. He doesn't usually take people under his wing like this."

Ariel gazed at me adoringly. "I can see that."

I'd had no shortage of admirers in my adult life—whether deserved or not, it comes with being wealthy—but knowing this young woman might see me as admirable made me feel a hell of a lot better about life in general.

Now, if I can manage to rein in my attraction for her, things just might be okay.

5
___

CHAPTER 5

Ariel

A couple of weeks had gone by with me trailing along after Francesca, the lead housekeeper. "Folding a fitted sheet is an art form, Ariel. Every good housekeeper knows how to execute this perfectly." She held a white sheet in front of her, then made some swift moves before putting the bundle—which now looked as if it had just come out of the package—down on the folding table. "Did you see what I did there?"

Shaking my head, I felt a little lost. "I did not," I admitted. "You went a little too fast for me."

With a heavy sigh that made her ample bosom heave, she picked up another sheet and went ten times slower. "Did you see what I did this time?"

"I did." I picked up a sheet and tried my hand at it. "Oh, now why is it not going into that position correctly?" I could feel her dark eyes boring into me. "And that's not right, either." I placed the thing on the folding table. "May I see you do it one more time, please? I'll get it. I promise."

"You made the rookie mistake of trying to fold it while it's right side out. You have to turn it inside out." Francesca showed me the inside seams, showing me how I should start. "See?"

"I do." I picked up my sheet to follow her lead. "Okay, inside out. There, I have it."

"Yes, that's great." She put her hands in two of the corners that were across from each other. "Like this, pull your hands until the corners have flattened out."

I copied her, but still had no clue how we were going to get to the next step. "Now what?"

She eyed me. "Pay close attention. It can get tricky here." She moved her right hand to join her left hand. "You will turn the corner right side out, combining the two corners into one nearly flat corner. You try it."

I did just as she'd done and accomplished the same thing. "Well, so far, so good."

"You notice the other corners that are hanging loose and still inside out, right?" she asked as she shook the sheet a bit to make them move.

"Yes, I see them." I watched her intently, not wanting to mess up after making it this far.

"Now you do the very same thing you did with the first two corners, adding each one over the last, turning it right side out." She went on to take the other corners in one at a time and ended up with all four corners aligned.

I managed to do the same, although mine wasn't as neat and tidy as hers was. "Okay, and now what?"

She placed the sheet on the folding table, so I did the same, still watching her hands intently so I didn't miss a step. "Now, you fold it. Let's hide the elastic by folding each edge inward."

I copied her. "There, that's starting to look right."

"It is." She smiled, making me feel proud. "Now all we do is fold this into a tidy rectangle. And we have our perfectly folded fitted sheet!"

As I made the last folds, I shouted, "Yes! I did it." Turning to her, I hugged her. "Thank you, Francesca!"

"I've never been hugged by anyone for showing them how to fold a sheet." She laughed as she patted my back. "You're welcome, Ariel."

"I've got the rest of these sheets. I want to practice until I can do them as quickly as you can." I set to work as she moved on to other tasks. "Am I silly for being so happy about learning something others would probably find a chore?"

"No, you're wonderful," she assured me. "It's a pleasure to have someone around who isn't grumbling about doing the work they're paid to do."

"I'm not much of grumbler, no matter the task." I thought better of that. "Except, I'm not fond of cleaning toilets. Not one bit."

"No one is," Francesca assured me.

That made me feel better. I didn't want to complain, but it was an unpleasant task. Not that I had any experience with it. Looking back, I realized that our father must've taken care of even that, never asking me or my mother to lift a finger. And yet our house—and toilets— had always been clean.

Lunchtime rolled around, and I found Mr. Dunne peeking into the laundry room. "Ariel, care to join me for lunch?"

He'd often asked me to join him for meals in those first two weeks of employment. I quite liked his company, so I took him up on his offer. "I would love to join you, Mr. Dunne. Where are we eating today?"

"I had lunch brought to my bungalow. I knew you had laundry this morning and thought you might like to take the hour off to rest your feet." Since the moment I'd met him, my boss had been nothing but thoughtful.

And then I noticed the sideways glance I got from Francesca. I knew he never invited any of the other housekeeping staff out for anything. I bit my lower lip as I looked at her, then back at him. "Perhaps Francesca would like to come, too?"

Before he could say a word, she said, "No, thank you. I'm meeting a friend of mine for lunch today."

"Well, that's nice," Mr. Dunne said. "Enjoy, Francesca." He waved at me. "Come with me, Ariel."

With my coworker not seeming to be bothered by my eating with our boss alone, I went to him. "What kind of food are you surprising me with today?"

His smile was on the devilish side. "Foie gras, among other things."

We walked side by side to his bungalow. "Sounds interesting. I'm sure I'll like it if you do. You have excellent taste."

"Glad you think so." He opened the door of his bungalow for me. "After you."

Our arms barely touched as I brushed past him. "Thank you, sir." A spark flowed through my body at the touch, reaching right down to my core. No matter how hard I'd tried to overcome the attraction I felt for him, it never went away. But I'd never said a single word about how he made me feel to anyone.

The sea breeze flowed through the living room through the opened doors that led to the deck. "I've had things set up out here on the deck, Ariel."

I saw that a table for two had been set up with white linens and a centerpiece made of shiny seashells with greenery billowing out of the vase. "Wow. How pretty is this?"

"Wish I could take the credit," he joked as he pulled out my chair. "Please, take a seat."

I did as he said, looking at the decadent foods spread out on various platters on the table. "Everything looks so delicious. I have no idea what most of these things are, but I'm sure I'll love it all."

"Love?" He chuckled, and it made his broad chest shake as he took his seat. "Love is a fleeting emotion, don't you think?"

I poured us both glasses of the red wine that sat in a chiller at one side of the table. "Fleeting, sir? Why would I think that?"

"Well, for instance, you might love the way a food tastes when you first eat it. Like the foie gras, for instance," he said. "This can either be an acquired taste or a taste one likes at first, but then grows tired of after a while. I've found that to be true about most things in life. Even romantic relationships."

"Are you saying that you've never been in love for an extended period of time?" I'd heard from some of my coworkers that he had never had a relationship of any substance. I couldn't help asking about him at any opportunity—he had captured my fascination from the first.

Nodding, he took a sip of wine. "I've found women I was attracted to—even women I liked so much I thought it might be love. But then something would happen. Not anything bad usually, just something that would turn my attention to something else. If love is real, then how would my attention turn so easily? And I don't mean from one woman to the next, either. I mean from a woman to maybe a project or a car. You know—anything else but her."

"Having never experienced love yet, I'm not in the position to take the opposite opinion of yours, Mr. Dunne. But I know my parents loved each other very much—maybe too much, seeing how things turned out for Mum and me—and I do like to believe that true love exists for everyone." It made me a little uneasy to think of Mr. Dunne with a woman, but I added, "And I hope you find the one woman meant for you someday, Mr. Dunne. It would be a shame if you didn't. You're a very nice man."

And nice looking, too.

My eyes went to my plate as I felt my body heat up.

Stop it!

He began spooning foods onto my plate as he smiled. "Thank you, Ariel. I'm glad you think I'm nice. I think you're nice, too. As a matter of fact, I was wondering if you feel you've been through enough training to start your position on my personal staff yet."

"There's so much to learn." I took a bite of the meat on my plate then moaned as it melted in my mouth. "Is this the stuff you were talking about?"

He nodded. "By the moan, I can see that you're one of those who love it at first bite—but mark my words, you'll tire of it eventually."

"I doubt I will." I took another bite. "It's so good."

"I bet you will." He took a bite, too. "I was one of those people who had to acquire a taste for it."

"But you love it now, don't you?" I stabbed a ripe strawberry, then popped it into my mouth.

"I like it very much." He grinned at me as he waved his fork at me, a blueberry stuck on the end of it. "I don't believe in love, remember?"

For some reason, his words bothered me. Not that they should've affected me at all, we weren't anything more than employer and employee.

My cell rang in my pocket, and I froze at the sound. "Oh, Lord."

Mr. Dunne got up, coming to my side as he held out his hand. "That call can only mean one thing. Let me take it for you, Ariel."

He was right. No one but the hospice had my number. And they'd been instructed to only call after her passing.

I handed him my cell after taking it out of my apron pocket. "Thank you, sir."

He put one hand on my shoulder as he answered the call, "Galen Dunne here. Have you news on Miss Pendragon's mother?" He was quiet for a moment, then said, "I see. Thank you very much. I will tell her right away."

He pulled off his sunglasses, putting them on the table along with my cell phone. I didn't need to hear him say it. "She's gone."

Slowly, he rubbed my shoulders and then pulled me up from my chair to hug me. The way his arms moved around my body, pulling me close, made me feel cared for. "Come here, sweetheart. Let me hold you, Ariel. Now is not the time to be alone."

Taking comfort in his arms, I let myself cry. I was now utterly alone in the world. But at least this wonderful man was here, showing he cared about me in my moment of grief.

I hope he never stops caring for me.

CHAPTER 6

Galen

Holding Ariel as she cried over her mother's passing, I felt a sense of rightness that I couldn't deny. I knew in that moment that I would be there for her no matter what. "Ariel, it's going to be okay. I hope you know I will help you in any way I can. You won't be alone."

Pulling herself together, she choked back sobs as she pulled her head off my shoulder to look at me through teary eyes. Even filled with tears, her eyes were beyond beautiful. "I can't thank you enough, Mr. Dunne. To know I've got you in my corner means the world to me."

I felt she needed more than I'd given her. She had nothing at all now outside of this resort—no family, no possessions other than what we'd provided her with. She needed something of her own. "Ariel, I want to give you a home. A real home."

"You have, sir." She looked down as she pulled herself out of my arms. "I'll be okay."

My fingers trailed down her arms as she stepped back. I didn't want to stop touching her. But I knew what I wanted wasn't right. "I mean a home, Ariel. Not just a room with an attached bathroom. A bungalow that will be your very own."

Shaking her head, she said, "I've got nothing to fill a home with. The offer is beyond kind, sir, but I'm just not ready to have my own place yet."

"You are." I took her by the hand, leading her into the living area. I knew food wouldn't go well with her grief. "The bungalow I'll give you will already be filled with everything you'll need. I think having your own place will do you good. I'm not taking no for an answer." I helped her take a seat on the sofa. "Here, you sit down." I pulled the coffee table up close to her. "Put your feet up." Then I got her glass of red wine from the table and put it in her hands. "You sip on this. I'm going to call Nova to get things going."

She looked up at me with sorrow-filled eyes. "Mr. Dunne, you really don't have to do all of this."

"I know I don't have to." I leaned over to kiss her on the top of her head. "I want to. I want to see you in your own home."

She took a sip of the wine as I went to get her a box of tissues. The sad, appreciative smile she wore when she took the box from my hand made my heart melt.

"Thank you, sir." Dabbing at the corners of her eyes, she took a deep breath. "I knew this day was coming. I don't know why I let it get to me like this. I know my mother is in a much better place now, after all."

"You'll miss her." I picked up the phone to call Nova and get her to work. "Nova, I want the bungalow next to mine to be cleaned, and I want to make sure it's fully functional, filled with everything Ariel will need. I'm giving it to her. Her mother passed away today, and I don't want her to have to deal with sharing accommodations with anyone else."

"I'll get on that right away, sir. It'll be ready within a few hours," Nova assured me.

Satisfied that Nova would take care of everything, I sat down next to Ariel. She looked at me with glistening eyes as she took another sip of her wine. "I don't know what I would do without you," she whispered.

"I don't want you to think about that." All I wanted to do was help her. "Tell me about them, Ariel. I want to know about your parents. How did the three of you get along?"

Gulping, her hand flew to her chest. "Oh, I don't know, Mr. Dunne. This is a little too much to ask you to deal with. You're my boss. I don't think—"

I stopped her by placing one finger to her pink lips. "I'm more than just your boss. Surely you know that by now. Does a person who is only your boss ask you to join them for meals so often?"

She closed her eyes as she shook her head, making tendrils of her auburn hair break free from her braid. "My father had hair like mine. I look more like him than my mother. But I act more like her than I ever did him."

Relieved she understood me, I took her hand in mine, holding it to my chest. "And what was like?"

Her eyes opened as her lips pulled into a smile. "My mother was a sincere woman. Quiet, loyal, devoted to her family. She allowed my father to dote on her, but never anyone else. She wouldn't ask for help no matter how badly she or I needed it. I'm that way, too. If my circumstances weren't so dire, I never would've made that call to you. I did it for her. Mum couldn't find any peace, not until I told her what you had offered me. She told me to take your offer and never look back."

"And I'm glad she did." Pulling her hand up, I kissed the top of it. "I'm glad to have met you. I'm glad you've allowed me to help you."

Staring at her hand where I'd left the kiss, she sighed before looking into my eyes. "I am, too. I truly am. For the first time in my life, I've got a goal."

I had to laugh a bit. "I hope your goals reach farther than just becoming a maid."

She blinked then looked down. "It's silly, isn't it?"

"No." I took her by the chin, pulling her face back up. "It's honorable to work. No matter what the work is. What I want is for you to envision bigger goals. And with my help, you will attain them. Would you like to finish high school?"

Looking a little confused, she asked, "What good would that do me? And I'm not being sarcastic. Would it truly do me any good?"

"Education is always good." I had no idea how much the poor thing had been held back from the world. "My dear, how did your parents talk to you about your future?"

Shrugging, she admitted, "They didn't. Not until Mum got sick. Then she began to worry about my future." She laughed a bit. "Now that I look back at it, it's rather delusional. How could she think she was taking good care of me while living on the streets? How could my father have thought that not letting us do anything on our own would help us in any way?"

"I'm sure he meant well, but he must've been mistaken about what it meant to be a good husband and father," I offered. "Perhaps he had no father figure to show him what one is supposed to do?"

"Ah," she mused. "You're right. He had no family. He'd been raised in an orphanage from the time he was a small boy."

"So he must've thought that his job was to do everything for his wife and then his child." I felt good about helping her to see that. "The only thing about that is that it takes away from the ones under his protection. He never allowed you two to learn about taking care of yourselves."

"Today I realized that my father even took care of the housekeeping. My mother and I never scrubbed a toilet. He had to have been the one who kept the house tidy." Her eyes went wide, looking bewildered. "Can you imagine going to work all day only to come home to clean the house, do the laundry, and cook the evening meal? And all the while my mother and I read or watched the telly, never lifting a finger. And that was per his instructions. I feel terrible now. He did all that to care for us—to prove he loved us. And what did we do to prove we loved him?"

It sounded like her father had had his work cut out for him. "I'm not sure what to say, Ariel. I suppose you and your mother allowing him to do all of those things let him know you both loved him, in a way."

"Let him?" she asked with confusion. "I've never looked it that way before."

She clearly had no clue the kind of satisfaction one could get from looking after another—particularly those you cared deeply for. "Well, let's say I tried to do everything for you. What would you do?"

"Well, I think you rather did try that at first." She nodded as she thought back. "Like when you wanted me to start off here as only your guest until I'd dealt with my issues. And I didn't let you. I think—somewhere deep inside—that I didn't want to be taken care of anymore."

"But if your father had still been alive, before everything fell apart for you and your mum, you would've let him continue looking after you like he'd always done, I bet."

She frowned at that thought. "Maybe if I were the same person I'd been before he died. But I don't think I ever want to go back to being that person. That person didn't even realize how helpless she was—and look where that had gotten me." She looked resolved, and I couldn't help but feel proud of her.

We talked about her and her family some more, with her sharing stories of her mum through laughter and tears. I didn't realize that a couple of hours had passed until Nova gave a knock at my door. "Mr. Dunne, Ariel's bungalow is ready."

I got up to answer the door, opening it to see Nova smiling away. "Did you gather her things from her room in staff housing?"

"Of course, sir." Nova looked at the bungalow not twenty feet from mine. "Shall I show her to her new home?"

"I'll do that. Thank you, Nova." Closing the door, I went back to find Ariel standing out on the deck, leaning on the railing as she gazed out at the evening sky. "Your new home is ready for you."

She turned to look at me, wiping her eyes as she did. "My new home. That sounds odd."

"I hope you get used to it sooner rather than later." Taking her by the hand, I led her back into the house then over the walkway to her home. Opening the door, I inhaled the fresh scent. "Smells wonderful in here."

Ariel's hand began to shake in mine. "This is too much." She looked around the room, taking in everything. The doors to the deck were left open and the cool evening air flowed through them. "I can't."

I stopped her from pulling her hand away from mine and pulled her into my arms instead. "You can."

The way her eyes darted away from mine told me she was nervous. "I'll try. Thank you. I'm sorry for acting this way. You've given me so much."

I had so much more I wanted to give her. "Nova, I care for you. I want you to be happy. Thank you for sharing so much with me today. It's the best gift anyone has ever given me."

"Crying on your shoulder?" she asked as her eyes went wide. "Telling you what a messed up family I've come from? That's a gift to you? I'll have to try harder to come up with something better than that the next time I give you a gift." She smiled at me, a generous smile that showed how much she liked me.

Moving one hand to the back of her neck, I could only think of one thing she could give me that might surpass the hours we'd spent together. Holding her, leaning in closer, I moved slowly, enough to give her the chance to say no if she wanted.

Her lips parted a bit as she looked into my eyes. Then her eyes closed, and I took her lips with a soft kiss. Lightning flashed through me, like nothing I'd ever experienced before.

My blood ran hot in my veins as our kiss grew in intensity. When her arms slid up to run around my neck, I picked her up, walking with her to the bar then placing her on it.

Finally, I heard some voice from deep inside me whisper. Finally her.

7

CHAPTER 7

Ariel

Heat pulsed through me as Galen kissed me with a passion I'd never felt before. I'd been kissed before; I'd even had sex once. That guy and I had only been sixteen, and that experience wasn't anywhere near as hot as the kiss I shared with my boss.

Oh, Lord, he's my boss!

Placing my hands on his chest, I applied gentle pressure to get him to stop the kiss. He didn't seem ready to end it as he took my hands, moving them back to run around his neck as he groaned a bit.

His mouth took mine with ease. Our tongues moved in gentle waves together as our hands began to move over each other's bodies. My head felt so light—his touch intoxicated me, it seemed. I didn't think the tiny amount of wine I'd consumed could've been responsible for that.

Moisture pooled in my satin panties. My nipples became so hard they could've cut glass. I was sure he felt them pushing through my thin satin bra and cotton button-down shirt. He held me so close our bodies were flush against each other.

Galen Dunne was all man. More man than I had ever expected to be with in my life. Wealthy, over and above handsome, and sexier than should be legal, the man took control of me easily.

No wonder his yacht's called Lady Killer.

Galen Dunne had to be a ladies' man. He knew he could have any woman he wanted. But at that moment, he seemed only to want me. And that made me hot.

Pulling at my shirt, he untucked it from my shorts, pulling the tail out then moving his large hands underneath it. His palms caressed the skin on my back, and then he pulled me even closer, my knees parting.

My butt slid on the bar's granite surface until his swollen cock pressed against my pulsating center. A moan slipped out of my mouth, but his kiss ate it up before I could finish.

God, he knows how to kiss!

I was putty in the man's hands, and I knew it without a doubt.

Putty?

What does one do with putty? Anything they want.

Wrenching my mouth from his, I turned my head while pushing against his chest. "Stop."

Resting his forehead against mine, he grumbled, "Why do you want to stop? You can't tell me this doesn't feel good."

I had one card to play that I knew would stop him from arguing with me about anything at that moment. "My mother has just died. This seems inappropriate to me."

"Shit!" His hands slid out from under my shirt then he turned away, huffing with frustration. "I'm sorry. You're right."

I felt frustrated, too. But I would cool down, and that would go away. This was a dangerous game I was playing; I was already too willing to become whatever this powerful man wanted me to be with just one kiss. I couldn't have that. I'd barely started my new life, and I wasn't about to hand it over to him—or anyone else, for that matter. "I'm sorry. I shouldn't have let that get so far."

Plopping down on the sofa, he looked up at me, still sitting on the bar. "Do you like me, Ariel?"

I nodded, then began tucking my shirt back in. "I do like you, Mr. Dunne."

"Mr. Dunne?" he asked as he smiled at me and winked. "I think we've moved a bit past that, don't you? At least to first name territory."

"I don't know if that's a good idea." I hopped off the bar, my legs weak from everything that had happened between us. As I worked at staying upright, I caught his haughty expression—as if he knew he'd done that to me in such a short amount of time. I went to sit in the chair across from where he was sprawled out on the sofa. He looked inviting as hell, seemingly waiting for me to come to lie in his strong arms.

Where he can put me right back into that helpless state? No!

"Say it, Ariel Pendragon. Say my name. I want to hear it from those plump, sweet lips of yours. Lips that feel like satin pillows under mine," his words made a shiver run through me.

I wrapped my arms around myself. "Sir, that's inappropriate."

He moved to lie on his side, lifting his upper body up then leaning his cheek on his hand. "Inappropriate? I don't think that two people who like each other—who share an amazing attraction the way we do—should consider anything they do inappropriate. These aren't normal circumstances, Ariel. This kind of attraction doesn't happen every day. I know you're young and inexperienced, but I can change the latter for you. All you've got to do is let me. Now say my name."

"I'm not going to do that, sir." I knew he was being stubborn and domineering, but I still couldn't help the smile that crept over my lips. The fact that the man wanted me so badly did things to me that made it hard to stand my ground.

"Your smile betrays ya, my darling." He sat up, leaning his elbows on his knees then leaning his chin on his steepled fingers. "Perhaps you should explain to me why you don't want to act on this attraction we have. I would love to know what you're thinking."

"Love?" I raised one brow at him; how ironic that he would phrase it that way. "But you don't love anything. You merely like things—certain things, not all things—and even then, only temporarily."

"Ah." He kept his piercing eyes on me. "So that's the issue, is it? Love isn't a requirement for sex, darling. You don't need to wait for love to take hold before you seek the satisfaction of sex."

"I disagree." I wasn't about to let him talk me into seeing things his way.

"You're not a virgin," he stated flatly.

"And how would you know that?" I asked, as I hadn't told anyone a thing about my sexual history—what little of it there was.

"You didn't kiss like one, that's how I knew." He leaned back on the sofa, running his arm along the back of it. "You should come sit with me. We can talk right here, you know."

"You only want me where you can touch me." I wasn't falling for his game. "And how would you know what a virgin kisses like?"

"I've had a handful of them in my lifetime." He seemed proud of that, and it made me grimace. His sexy grin turned into a frown. "And that look is for what?"

"It's for the fact that you're proud of taking not one, but several girls' innocence—a gift—and giving them nothing in return." I found it disgusting and selfish that he would gloat about such a thing.

"They got plenty in return. Don't you worry your sweet mind about any of them. They weren't crying when I left them, if that's what you're thinking. We all parted ways amicably." He moved his arm off the back of the sofa, placing his hand on his upper thigh. It was very close to the still swollen bulge beneath his khaki shorts.

I pulled my eyes up from the lump near his hand to look into his eyes. "Or to be more honest, you parted ways when you found something else that interested you more and moved on."

"But the thing that matters is that no one was hurt by a thing. And neither will you. Trust me." He wiggled his finger at me. "Come on, come sit by me."

"I think that would be a terrible idea." His unending gaze made me fidget in the chair. "As it is, everyone I work with thinks our spending time together is unorthodox. And now you've given me a bungalow all to myself. One right next door to you no less. I expect tongues will be wagging about the two of us."

"And your point is?" he asked as he smiled at me.

"My point is that I won't be doing what they think we're doing. I want to focus on doing what I came here to do—work and get paid and make my own life. My life, Mr. Dunne. Not a life where you get to control me and what I do."

"Control you?" His eyes held pain just then, and it hurt me to see it. "I'm not trying to do any such thing, Ariel. I swear to you that I'm not. That's not who I am as a person. I have no intentions of making you do anything you don't want. Not even have sex with me. I think we'd have off-the-charts great sex, and I'd like nothing more than to get to doing that, but I have no desire to control you at all. Only spend time with you. And if some of that time could be spent in the sack, then that's all the better. If you know what I'm saying?" He winked.

"Yes, I completely understand what you're saying. You want to make love to me," I used that term on purpose. I knew it would get to him.

The way he narrowed his eyes told me it had worked. "I want to have sex with you. Making love is for starstruck, misled softies, which I am not."

"Maybe I am." All this banter was making me thirsty, so I stood up and headed to the fridge. "I hope there are bottles of water in here. I'm thirsty. Would you care for a bottle of water, sir?"

My back to him, I had no idea he'd gotten up and followed me. His hands on my waist, his breath on my neck, made me stop. The incredible sensation made me lean back against his broad chest and sigh. I could feel his lips curve into a satisfied smile. "See, you like me."

"I never said I didn't." I put my hands over his where they were wrapped around my waist. "I don't want to be your plaything."

"Why not?" he chuckled, making us both shake as his chest rumbled. "Being my plaything can be lots of fun. Let's have fun, you and I. I will give you exclusivity if you'd like."

Turning to face him, I had to ask, "And what does that mean, exactly?"

"So long as we're doing the deed, we will not see other people."

He kissed the tip of my nose. "I'm not a monster, Ariel. I only have one woman at a time. I'm not quite the player you must think I am."

"Doing the deed," I whispered. "You make it sound so inviting." I rolled my eyes at him, turned and slipped out of his arms. "I'll not settle for that, Mr. Dunne."

"Just say my name one time, Ariel. Damn, it's not that hard to do." He hopped up to sit on top of the bar.

I grabbed two bottles of water out of the stocked fridge then handed one to him before stepping back a couple of paces. "I don't see what good that would do, sir. If you think I'll say your name and magically become enamored with you and be willing to become your..." I searched for the appropriate words to describe what type of relationship he wanted and could only come up with one vulgar phrase, "...fuck buddy, then you're in for quite the shock."

"I'm forty-one, Ariel. Not exactly a kid. And not exactly the type of man who has a fuck buddy." His eyes turned stern. "I am a man. You are a woman. A gorgeous, sassy, sweet woman who has my dick in a tizzy."

Gasping at his confession, I felt heat pooling in my panties once more. "Oh Lord!"

"Yes, oh Lord." He got off the bar then came toward me. I felt frozen in place, skewered by his eyes, which never left mine. They seemed to hold me perfectly still for him. "I want you, Ariel. I want you more than I've ever wanted anyone. And that's the truth. I can take you to places you've never been, both physically and mentally. I can make you see God, Ariel. Let me do that for you."

"And you think I can do the same for you?" I knew I had some power over him. If he wanted me, he could have me. But only if he wanted all of me—heart and body.

"I'm sure you could." He moved forward so slowly—it almost seemed as if he wasn't moving at all. "Let this happen. Let us find comfort in each other. You won't be sorry. I promise you that you will never be sorry you did this."

"If I did this without love involved, I would be sorry, sir." My palms were flat against the stainless steel surface of the refrigerator as

I tried to stand my ground even though my back was proverbially, and literally, against the wall. "I did that once before and vowed I would never do it again. You can't just pick and choose which parts of me you'll have. If you want me, it's all or nothing. I won't shortchange myself again."

He took three steps back, but his eyes never left mine. "Tell me about your sexual experiences that have made you build this shield around yourself."

Talking about my terrible sexual experience wasn't something I wanted to do with him. "I'd rather not."

Slipping to one side, I made my way back to my chair, grabbing the bottle of water off the counter as I went. He stayed right where he was.

As I took my seat, I didn't like the way he had his back to me. And it occurred to me rather suddenly that he might just walk out the door and leave me. And I didn't really want to be alone. But I didn't say a thing to him.

His head fell forward, and he put his face in his hands. "I'm an ass."

I didn't know how to respond to that, so I just waited to see what ploy he was working on now. I couldn't stop watching him as he stood there with his face in his hands. When he slowly pulled his head up, dropped his hands to his side, then walked forward to open the fridge, I had no idea what he was doing.

He pulled out a carton of eggs and a package of bacon. Without saying another word, he started to take pots and pans out from the cabinets, and in no time there was the smell of bacon in the air. He even made a pot of coffee, all without saying a word.

When he was finished, he plated up the food on two plates, poured cups of coffee for us, then put it all on the small dining room table. Only then did he come to me, reaching his hand out for me to take. "You need to eat something. You were right; your mother has just passed, and this isn't the best time for this conversation. Come, I've made scrambled eggs, bacon, and toast for you. It will all be easy on your stomach. I'm sure it's delicate right now, with both your grief and what I've just put you through. I hope you can forgive me."

"No need to apologize, Mr. Dunne. There is something between us, after all. I do know that, too." I took his hand and let him lead me to the small table for two. "This looks great. Thank you. I'm not feeling very hungry, but you're right, I do need to eat something, or I'll make myself sick. And thank you for sharing this meal with me. It's very nice of you."

He nodded as he took a seat across from me. "It is very nice, isn't it? Apparently, I can be a nice man when I want to be."

Nicer than he probably realized—most of the time.

CHPATER 8

Galen

S itting alone on my deck, I watched the moon's glow over the water and wondered when I'd lost my touch—and then I wondered when I'd lost my mind.

Ariel had just gotten the news that her mother had passed, and I'd used that time to make my move on her.

What the fuck was I thinking?

There was a part of me that thought we'd fall to the floor in a heap of flesh, taking what we needed from each other in a flurry of sexual positions that would make whoever wrote the Kama Sutra blush. Obviously that hadn't happened. I hadn't expected her to completely pull away from me the way she had.

I was ashamed that it had taken so long for my libido to step back and my heart to step in. She'd just lost her mother. She wasn't in her right mind. She needed a friend, not a lover.

At least I'd turned around and done the right thing eventually. I'd made her a simple meal then cleaned up after we ate, and then I left her alone to give in to her grief.

I should've let her do that in the first place, but I'd been engulfed with desire for some reason. It had made me selfish, and I was ashamed of my actions.

Picking up my nearly empty glass of Scotch, I heard the sound of soft footsteps coming up behind me. "I wanted to tell you thank you, Mr. Dunne."

My cock jerked at the mere sound of her voice. Stop it!

She's come to say thank you, nothing more than that.

"You're welcome," I said without turning to look at her. I knew that seeing her beautiful face, her gorgeous body—which was round in all the right places—and those devastating eyes would do me in. "Night."

"Okay." I heard her steps retreating. "Night, sir."

That was it. I couldn't take it anymore. "Damn it, Ariel, call me Galen!" I snapped.

"No, thank you." The sound of her footsteps got faster, and then I heard the front door of my bungalow closing.

She was being timid, and I was getting tired of it. At only twenty-one, I knew her age and inexperience was something I would have to work around. I had no idea how hard it would be though.

I went to take a shower after that. The frustration was too much to bear, and I knew I had to get some relief or I would make even bigger mistakes when I saw her the next morning for her first day of cleaning my place.

The warm water flowed over my bare skin as I closed my eyes and reached down to cup my balls, imagining it was her hand instead of my own. They were full, heavy, and needed to be drained desperately.

Her voice came from the other side of the bathroom door, "Galen, can I come in?"

Gulping, I couldn't believe she'd come. "Yes."

Stepping into the dimly lit bathroom, Ariel wore only a white robe, which she quickly dropped, her nude body luminous in the scant light. "I'm sorry about earlier, Galen. I want you."

"I'm glad you've come to your senses, Ariel." I moved back as she stepped into the shower. "Now let me show you how great we can be together."

Her hands ran over my six-pack, then up to my pecs as she bit her lower lip. "You're so muscular, Galen. I want to kiss every last inch of you."

"Please do." I leaned back against the warm tiled wall as she kissed a trail up the line that separated my abs. Her red nails raked over my nipples, making them spring to life as I groaned at the sensation. "Yes, Ariel. Touch every part of me. Leave your marks all over my body, then I'll do the same to yours."

Her tongue slid back down the line she'd just kissed, and then she went to her knees. Her auburn hair was soaked and slicked back as she looked up at me, then cupped my balls in one hand. "Can I kiss you here?"

"Yes," I moaned as she pursed her pink lips, then placed them on the tip of my erection.

Her mouth opened, and she slid it all the way down the length of my cock as she played with my balls. Expertly, she moved her head back and forth as she let the tip of her tongue glide along the bottom of my shaft with each stroke. With one long suck, she opened her green eyes and looked up at me, lips wrapped perfectly around me.

Gazing into those deep orbs of hers, I coached her, "A little slower, baby. Make it last. Daddy doesn't want to get off too soon."

She slowed down and closed her eyes, then moaned, the vibration stirring me to my core. She pulled her mouth away just before I was about to come and slid her body up mine, moving her hands to grip my shoulders. "I'm ready for you to fuck me now, sir."

Lifting her up, I eased my hard cock into her hot cunt as we both moaned with relief to finally be connected. "Fucking you is as close to heaven as I've ever been, baby." I moved back and forth then pinned her back to the wall so I could go harder. "You like the way I fuck you?"

"Oh, yes, Daddy. Fuck me hard. Make me yours. I've never had such a big dick inside of me before." She squealed with desire as I plunged into her harder and harder.

Her nails dug into my back as she mewed with pleasure. "You like

Daddy's big cock in you, huh? You want me to fuck you all night long, don't you, you little slut?"

"Yes, fuck me all night long. I'm your slut, Daddy. Yours and no one else's. This pussy was meant for you and only you. I wish I'd saved it for you." She growled then bucked to meet my savage thrusts. "Fuck me! Harder, harder!"

"You're so much naughtier than I gave you credit for." Moving my finger that gripped her hip, I circled the little pucker of her asshole before shoving it in, making her cry out. Her body shook, and her cunt clamped down on my cock, giving me no mercy as she exploded around me. "Come for me, you little slut. Come all over Daddy's cock!"

"Ah!" she screamed as she let it all go. I shot into her, making her even more slippery, and I kept pumping into her with all I had in me. "Oh, Daddy, give me all you've got. I want it all. Fuck me. Oh, take me any way you want. I'm your slut. Your whore. I'm whatever you need me to be."

The loud sound of panting and growling filled my ears, and I opened my eyes to find thick strands of white come going down the shower drain. "Shit! God damn it!"

I was alone. Ariel hadn't been there at all.

Even more disappointing than the fact that the hottest fantasy I'd ever had was just that—a fantasy—was the fact that our status wasn't anywhere other than where we'd been before I hopped in the shower. My hand was still wrapped around my spent cock, and I let it go, feeling less fulfilled than a good fantasy and self-stimulation usually got me.

I needed her. I needed the real woman. If I didn't get her, then I didn't know what I would do. I needed to feel her soft body in my arms. I needed to be inside of her like I needed air to breathe.

Getting out of the shower, I wrapped a towel around my waist then went to bed. Dropping onto it, I looked up at the ceiling and gave myself a talking to. "She can't be what you want her to be, Galen. She won't be your slut, and you know that. She'll demand more out of you than that."

But that was the only kind of sex I ever had. Nasty, dirty sex with women who got off on being naughty. Even the virgins had had those tendencies. I'd just gotten to them before they gave it to someone else.

Ariel was furthest thing from a naughty girl I could image. She was a good girl. A very good girl who I wanted to turn into a sex-hungry slut. I wanted her to want to give me whatever I asked for. I wanted her to be my whore, and I wanted her to want that, too.

But I knew now that she would never spread her legs for me when I snapped my fingers the way all the others did. Without any doubt, I knew Ariel wasn't like the rest of the women I'd have sex with.

Ariel would never be with me unless she could have my heart and trust me with hers. And that wasn't a thing I wanted or needed.

The woman was frail. Her mother had just passed, and yet there I was, fantasizing about taking her in the roughest, dirtiest way, and wanting with everything in me for it to be real.

I'm a beast, and she deserves better than a beast.

CHAPTER 9

Ariel

S itting on the deck of my bungalow, chills of excitement ran through me. This is my place. All mine.

I'd never had my own place, and not even in my craziest fantasies had I imagined having one this nice. And I had Mr. Dunne to thank for that.

I was still feeling conflicted about what had happened between us earlier. There was no doubt there was heat between us, but it was a heat I needed to dampen. I never wanted to leave the island or my job, and I didn't want to compromise my position here by messing around with the boss. I knew I needed to let him know that there was no chance that I would be moving into a sexual relationship with him. If I didn't nip this in the bud right away, then I might not get to have my happily ever after ending I'd been given a chance at.

Aside from the conflict that would arise, I also didn't want my coworkers thinking of me as nothing more than a common whore if I started having sex with our boss. I had already noticed some people cutting me sideways looks. Giving them proof of what they already suspected would end in disaster.

With my legs dangling over the side of the deck, I sipped on coffee, trying to prepare myself for the day. Mr. Dunne had told me that I would no longer need any more training, and that I would start that very day as his personal maid.

I didn't know how I was going to have a civil conversation with the man without bruising his ego—an ego I knew was inflated by past experiences with far too many women.

He'd be disappointed with me anyway.

After I went to his bungalow to say thank you for the meal he'd made me, I returned home and found a laptop computer in my bedroom on the desk. It was then that I decided to look up my employer.

There was one picture after another of Galen with different beautiful women hanging on his arm. And every woman in every picture wore one of those disarming, seductive smiles. A smile I knew I'd never be able to give.

He had a definite type.

I didn't want to, nor did I even think I could do what that man would expect in the bedroom. And he needed to know that. The sooner the better, I thought.

Getting up, I picked up my coffee cup, then went inside to clean up before heading next door to get to work. From what I'd glimpsed of his place the day before, it wasn't in bad condition. But there would be cleaning to do nonetheless. If he wanted any meals, I'd had to cook for him as well.

Putting on a perky attitude, I went out the door then walked across the walkway to his door. A quick rap, then I waited.

"Is that you, Ariel?" he asked from inside.

"It is, sir."

"Well, come in. No need to knock, my dear."

I found the door unlocked, then opened it and went inside. He sat in a high-backed chair with a white robe on, reading a newspaper. Steam drifted up from a white coffee cup that sat on the end table to his left.

"Good morning, sir. Have you eaten yet?" I asked as I walked into the kitchen. And then I saw the pan in the sink and knew his answer. "Oh, looks like you have. I'll just get this cleaned up. Will you be wanting me to prepare your lunch or dinner today? I'd just like to know how I should schedule my day."

"I won't be around, Ariel. I'll leave you to your work today and stay out of your way." He got up, put the paper on the chair then walked toward his bedroom. "Don't throw the newspaper away. Place it on the rack with the others, please."

I should've been overjoyed. The man was finally treating me as his employee. However, the overwhelming emotion I felt was confusion.

But I didn't say anything as I washed the pan, then found the cleaning supplies underneath the sink and got to work. Silently, I cleaned the kitchen then caught a glimpse of Mr. Dunne as he came out of his bedroom.

He was wearing a suit that his thick fingers were finishing buttoning up. "And where are you off to, sir?" I had no right to ask and knew that.

"Aruba." He looked around for something, and I spotted his cell phone on the coffee table.

I went to fetch it. "You'll need this then, won't you, sir?"

"I will." He smiled as he took it out of my hand. Our fingers barely touched, yet I still felt a twinge in my nether regions. "I was looking for that, thank you, Ariel."

"You're very welcome, sir." I turned away to attempt to get a hold of myself. The doors to the deck were open, and I took in a deep breath of fresh air.

"It's nice out, isn't it?" he asked from right behind me.

"It is." I took a couple of steps away from him before turning around to face him. "But isn't it always nice out here in paradise?"

"Most of the time it is." He looked past me, out at the sea. "When storms come up, it can be a bit frightening. But that doesn't happen often."

"Should I wash your sheets?" I asked him as I tried not to look at how damn handsome he was in that black suit.

"If you want to." He walked over to pick up his coffee cup, then took it to the sink where he turned the faucet on to rinse it out. "I've got a meeting in Aruba today. I have no idea when I'll get back here. Don't lock up if I'm not home before you leave. There's no crime on the island, so security's not an issue. I never lock up anything here."

My heart stopped as I wondered what kind of person he was meeting, male or female. I didn't want to sound weird, but had to ask —even though I had no right. "Oh, and who is this person you're meeting with, Mr. Dunne?"

"Priscilla Bowling," he answered me, making my heart ache. "She's the headmistress of an all-girl school in Scotland. She'd like to make some much-needed improvements to the school and hasn't gotten all the funding she needs. I'm meeting with her so I can see if I want to add to her funds or not."

It sounded like something that could've been handled over the phone, and the words spilled out before I could think better of it. "Is that really something you need to go over in person? You should watch yourself, Mr. Dunne. You don't want to get taken." Somehow my mouth just kept on moving. "And an all-day meeting? Sound pretty intense for something that could likely be sorted out through e-mail or over the phone." With a sigh, I finally shut my lips tightly.

This is none of my concern. I am his maid and nothing more.

"Well, then maybe you should join me to make sure I don't get taken, Miss Pendragon." I turned to looked at him and was met with his smile.

"You're joking." I picked up the can of wood polish and a cloth and went to clean the end table, which now had a ring where his cup had been. "I'm sorry for putting in my two cents. I don't know what I was thinking. You have a nice day, sir."

"I'm serious, Ariel. Come with me." He reached out, putting his hand on my wrist. "I would appreciate the company. You can come along as my assistant, not my maid."

"I'm not qualified for that." I shook my head. I'd finally gotten what I wanted with him treating me like his maid, and now I was falling back into the pit of the attraction that kept disrupting my good sense. "I know my place, sir."

With a huff, he wrapped his fingers around my wrist, then pulled me to him. "Your place is wherever I say it is." His eyes pierced mine, then they closed, and he let me go. "I am sorry. I should go. I don't know why I keep doing this to you. I truly don't. I will stop it, though. I promise you that I will."

I didn't want him to stop. As much as I kept telling myself that I wanted him to treat me like an employee, a huge part of me didn't truly mean it. "I'm a bit broken, Mr. Dunne."

He stopped his retreat to turn to look at me. "I'm aware of that, Miss Pendragon. That's precisely why I must get a hold of myself, because you're a good woman."

His words made me feel a bit confused. "A good woman, sir?"

The way his chest moved as he chuckled held my attention. The memory of how it felt to be against that same chest as it moved flooded my mind. My knees went weak, and I had to lean on the chair to steady myself.

"I've been treating you poorly." He walked toward me, closing the distance between us until he could reach out. His knuckle grazed my cheek. "I've let lust come between us. You aren't a woman who should merely be lusted after. Unfortunately, that is all I have to give."

I was silent a moment, trying to figure out how to put the words together to tell him my story. "A man grabbed me once while Mum and I were sleeping in an alley off Piccadilly Circus. He managed to throw me over his shoulder and carry me away to another alley where he slammed my body against the wall, then pushed my skirt up."

Mr. Dunne's face went pale. "You don't have to tell me this, Ariel."

"I think I do, sir." I gulped back the familiar knot that formed in my throat every time I thought of that horrid night. "He moved his finger over my privates as he blew his stinking breath in my face. He told me to call him Master. He told me he'd go easy on me if I just did what he said—whatever he said—for he'd give me many demands.

He told me I would be his whore, and he would sell me to whomever he liked, and that I would thank him for it."

Mr. Dunne fell into the chair, his color ashen and his mouth agape. "Ariel, I am so sorry."

"I didn't tell you to make you feel sorry for me, sir. I told you so you could understand that I am not one to play games when it comes to sex. I do not want to be toyed with. Sex isn't just sex to me. Sex can be used to hurt people. But making love...now, that can be a beautiful thing shared by two people who are committed to each other." I balled my fist at my side then swiped it through the air. "Thankfully, I slammed my fist into that wretched man's face, kneed him in the groin, and then punched him in the stomach. He let go of me just long enough for me to run back to my frightened mum, who held me and told me how glad she was that I was safe."

His blue eyes held mine. "You are truly remarkable, Ariel Pendragon. A rare woman indeed."

I could see the admiration in his eyes, but it was tempered by something I wouldn't have expected. He almost looked afraid.

CHAPTER 10

Galen

After hearing Ariel's story, I backed off completely. Still treating her as a friend, I stopped trying to bait her as I had with the whole fake meeting with another woman thing, which I knew would spark jealousy.

It had done that, and it had also led her to tell me about her horrible experience from when she lived on the streets of London. I couldn't shake the feeling her story had given me.

Ariel wasn't only a good woman with strong convictions, but she was strong and tough, too. She was so full of perseverance that it was easy to forget that she'd lived a difficult, unconventional life. There was no doubt in my mind that she would never succumb to any of the pressure or charms I laid on her unless love was a part of it.

Not knowing what the future would hold for us, I wanted Ariel to have the independence she deserved. So I did something I thought would see to that. I'd made a substantial deposit into her bank account along with her weekly pay.

She'd been working for a month and had done well. I planned on calling it a bonus when she asked, which I knew she'd do.

My heart raced as she came into my bungalow after taking a short break to go to her place, and she marched straight out to me on the deck. I knew she must have checked her bank account as it was payday. What I didn't expect was such a horrible scowl on her pretty face. "What is this?" She wagged a paper in the air.

I assumed it was a print out of her bank statement. But I pretended I had no idea. "What is what, my dear?"

"This," she shrieked, then slammed the paper on the table in front of me.

"Do you see that there, Mr. Dunne? That amount?"

I looked at the six-digit number, then gave her a smile. "Oh, that. It's a bonus for all your hard work."

"No!" She slammed her fist on top of the paper. "That is a disgrace is what that is. I shouldn't be getting a bonus yet anyway. Do you think I haven't spoken with the other employees here, Mr. Dunne? We get a bonus at Christmas and one at the end of the summer, and that's all."

"Well, none of them are my personal maid." I took her by the wrist to make her stop throwing her hands around. "Ariel, stop. I wanted you to feel secure and independent. That's all this is about."

"I want to make that money myself. I want to earn it. I don't want it handed to me." She tugged her hand away from my grip. "My father just about crippled me with all of his help. I will never be treated that way again. Even if you have the best of intentions, Mr. Dunne, I won't be crippled again."

I hadn't realized I was doing anything like that. "I am sorry, Ariel. I didn't think you would take it that way."

"Well, I did. And I can't see how you thought I would take it any differently." She put her hands on her hips, shifting her weight to one foot. "I've told you everything about my father and how he treated us. And I don't hate him for any of it, but I won't fall into that again."

She was right, and I knew it. "I'll take the extra money back. And I'll try to think things through better where you're concerned."

"I know I seem difficult to you." She turned to walk away from me. "But that's just who I am."

"No, you're not being difficult. I'm the one who's doing things wrong. I should've remembered the things you've told me." I had miscalculated, and I could take the blame. "How about you let me make it up to you?"

She spun around to look at me with her mouth gaping. "Now why would you feel that you've got anything to make up for? You gave me an exorbitant amount of money. I told you I wouldn't accept it. You said you would take it back. The issue has been resolved, sir. No need to make anything up to me." Picking up the bucket with the mop in it, she headed to clean the bathroom. "I'll be finishing up for today now."

Such pride, such passion for holding her own and carrying her own weight. I was hard-pressed to think of anyone else I knew with so much integrity. I found a smile that would not leave my face and got up to go inside, taking the paper with me.

Since I felt I needed to do it quickly, I got out my laptop and cancelled the money transfer, putting it back into my account. I'd paid her with my own money, not the resort's. If she'd have known that, she would've really blown a gasket.

I had to watch myself with the girl. She was full of surprises. Not that I was complaining. Even though I could see that she thought of herself as a problem, she was anything but that. To me, at least, she wasn't a problem at all—she was remarkable.

As I sat at the desk in the living area, I saw Ariel come out of my bedroom then go out on the deck to rinse out the mop and toss the dirty water into the sea. After doing that, she stood there, looking out at something. She took her cell out of her pocket then took a few pictures of what I now saw were seabirds drifting just above the surface of the clear water.

Putting the phone back in her pocket, she turned and caught me watching her. "Hold it." She pulled the phone back out and took a picture of me. "There. Now I've got one of you. My angel. You brought me to paradise and turned my life around in a way I never could've imagined, not even in my craziest dreams." Her smile gave me goosebumps. "Thank you for all you've done, sir. Never think you need to do anything more for me. I'm forever in your debt as it is."

"No, you are not in my debt." It made me angry that she even thought that. "You have a job, you do that job very well, and that means you've earned everything you've been given. I don't want you to thank me for anything more than this opportunity you were given —which you've done well with. You did this, Ariel. I'm so proud of you. You really have no idea how proud I am."

With a shrug, she put the phone back in her pocket. "I don't know why you should be any more proud of me than you are of anyone else who works here for you. We all try our hardest."

She didn't even see it. That's what made her so damn special. Not one of my other employees on that island had her unique and harsh past. To me, she was so far above them, and she had no clue.

It had been some time since she and I had dined out together. After our recent awkwardness, I think we both thought it would be a bad idea. But I wanted to do something special with her. "Yes, you all do your very best here. It's appreciated. What do you say to joining me for dinner out this evening in Aruba? We can get cleaned up, hop on the yacht, then head over that way."

As I knew she would, she shook her head. "I don't think that's a good idea."

"Well, you should." I'd come up with an idea that would definitely work. "Because I want your help in planning an employee appreciation day that we'll all spend in Aruba. We can check out the casinos and hotels and find out which are the best. Together, we'll set up a night out for all those who bust their collective butts for this resort."

Smiling at me, she nodded. "I can do that. Let me just get changed, and I'll meet you at the dock." She skipped away to go to her bungalow, and I laughed as I watched her go.

Not much later she and I were on the yacht, heading to Aruba. "Now, I don't want you to tell a soul about what we're doing. I want this to be a surprise."

Ariel placed her hand on my arm as we stood next to each other on deck, the wind whipping through our hair. "I thought as much. I won't tell anyone." She looked over her shoulder then back at me. "And what does the crew think we're going to Aruba for?"

"Promise not to get mad at me?" I asked, as I had something I wanted to test with her.

"Sure, why not?" she asked. "What did you tell them?"

"I told them that you and I were going on a date." I watched her eyebrows climb up her forehead. And I knew some angry words were about to pop out of her pretty mouth. "Just kidding. You should've seen your face." I laughed at seeing the reaction I was sure I'd get from her.

Shaking her fist at me, she said, "You're such a joker, Mr. Dunne." Dropping her fist, she looked a little funny as she said, "One of the other maids asked me something the other day when we were in the laundry room together."

"What was that?" I had a pretty good idea but wanted to be sure.

"She asked if you and I were getting romantic with each other." She blushed. "I told her that we weren't doing anything like that. And do you know what she said to me, Mr. Dunne?"

I had a good idea again, but feigned ignorance. "I've got no clue, Ariel. What did she say?"

"She said that she's seeing Roger from groundskeeping." Ariel looked a little shocked by that. "And she also told me that Francesca is seeing Joel from accounting. The man who makes her paychecks. Can you believe that?"

I laughed. "Ariel, the island is small. Of course there will be affairs among the staff. And sometimes there have been affairs with the staff and the guests. It's natural, if you really think about it."

Slipping my arm around her shoulders, I looked out at the sunset as it melted into the water behind the yacht. "You live in paradise, Ariel. You really should try to enjoy it more."

She looked at me with a funny expression. "Maybe you're right."

"I'm always right." I looked at her. "Well, most of the time I'm right," I had to correct myself. I'd done and said more wrong things to that woman than I had in my entire life. "I'm right about this. How about that?"

She nodded then put her head on my shoulder. "Sometimes I think about our lives, Mr. Dunne. One of us was born for greatness, and one was born to be a pauper. How is that?"

"First of all, you were not born to be a pauper. That was thrust upon you by circumstances that were somewhat out of your control." I hugged her a little. "And I wasn't born into greatness. I made greatness happen for me. And you can, too. There is nothing holding you to your place right now. You don't have to be a maid forever. You can grow, too. You can grow as much as you want. It's all up to you now. There is nothing limiting you in any way."

Her eyes bore into mine. "I do feel limited right now though—that there are things stopping me from having everything I want in life. Why do you think that is?"

I had a very good idea why she felt limited. She wanted something that she thought she would never get. My heart. But I didn't mention that.

"I think you need to spread your wings some more so that you know you can fly. Then you won't feel those limitations anymore."

"And what about you, sir?" she asked with a sexy grin. "How about your wings? Should you spread them, too?"

Maybe I should.

CHAPTER 11

Ariel

A few days later, after our trip to Aruba, I found myself alone in my bungalow. Searching for the right way to handle my thoughts about Galen, I looked up at the sky for help from above. "My head tells me to watch out, that the man isn't the commitment type. It also tells me that I have a secure job, my own home, and a future at the resort. If I give in to this shared attraction, then I might well be giving up this incredible life and security I've stumbled upon."

Only the seagulls chirped back at me. Turning to head back inside my bungalow, I nearly tripped over one of my discarded sandals.

As I bent over to pick it up, I saw a small shadow dashing through the living area. Grabbing the shoe, I held it at the ready to defend myself against whatever had barged into my home.

An odd chattering met my ears, and the sound had me lurching forward into the house to see what had gotten inside. "Out! Get out! Whatever you are, you've got to go."

The front door opened a bit, letting a stream of light shoot through the living area. And then I saw what had entered my home—the same thing that was exiting quickly, chittering all the way out.

A monkey?

Running to close the door behind the intruder, I pushed the door closed then locked it up tightly. Only then did I hear Galen calling from across his deck beside mine, "Ariel, did I hear you shouting at someone? Are you okay?"

Going back out onto the deck, my sandal still in my hand, I found myself panting. "Yes, I'm okay. Mr. Dunne, were you aware that there are monkeys on this island?"

"Monkeys?" Leaning over to look at me, Galen seemed confused. "No. I've never seen a monkey here, Ariel. Are you sure you saw that right?"

"It had a little white cap of hair on top of its head. And beady little black eyes and sharp white teeth." Or had it? I wasn't so sure now. I'd had such a short glimpse of it that I questioned whether the creature might've been distorted in my imagination. "Anyway, it was a monkey. I'm getting on my computer right now to see what kind it is."

"I doubt you saw an actual monkey." Galen laughed, then jerked his head to one side. "You want me to come take a look around for you?"

Being alone with Galen—outside of work hours—was a situation I'd been trying desperately to avoid. His eyes, his body, his scent alone sent me into a state that I knew one day I wouldn't be able to fight any longer. "No. I'm sure I've scared it off for now. But you should alert security so they can find it and take care of it."

"You mean, you want them to kill the monkey?" Galen asked with a stunned expression.

"No." I didn't mean that at all. "I meant to take it to a zoo or something."

"There are no zoos anywhere around here." He cocked his head then winked at me. "What do you say we just let the little thing run free?"

"Then I think we will have a reason to lock our doors, Mr. Dunne. My front door was shut but it seems to have turned the handle and strolled right in. It would be a fright to wake up one night with a growling monkey on your chest." I tossed the shoe into the house, then took a seat on the deck. "My door is locked now, but I bet you can't say the same for yours. He's on the loose, you know, the little trespasser."

The way the man stood there smiling at me as if I were crazy should've made me angry. But he was too damn cute to get mad at. And then his head turned as I heard a slam from inside his home. "Shit!"

All I could do was laugh as he left his deck in a hurry. But my laughter changed in a heartbeat as I heard crashing and shouting. Jumping up, I ran through my home and to the kitchen pantry, grabbing a broom and then headed for the door.

Sprinting to the bungalow next door, I found the door open and headed in. "I'm here to help, Mr. Dunne. Run it my way, and I'll use the broom to sweep it out of here."

"He's a fast one, Ariel. Watch out, he's coming your way! I heard him call out from the bedroom." The monkey's chatter filled the air as he headed toward me, and I held the door open, using the broom to help the thing on his way out. The little creature stopped to turn and glare at me for ruining his fun, but then he hurried away. I watched him as he scurried to the line of trees where the jungle began, and then he disappeared.

"I think he's gone home now," I whispered as I kept a close eye on where he'd entered the jungle.

A hand on my shoulder made everything inside of me heat up, then melt. "Thanks for the help. I hadn't counted on it since I'd teased you about the thing."

"It's what any good neighbor would do." I moved, stepping out the door, away from his touch. "Maybe we scared the thing. Maybe he'll stay where he belongs."

He grabbed my arm, stopping my retreat. "How about you and I go down to Cantina Cordova and have a cocktail or two? It's your day off. You might as well do a little something more than sit on your deck all day."

I didn't think that would be a good idea. "I can't. I've got my own house to clean today." It wasn't even dirty, but I had to come up with some excuse.

"Hmm." He let me go. "Still afraid, I see."

I didn't like him thinking that I was afraid of him. "Look, you and I see things very differently. That day, when we went to Aruba, you told me to spread my wings. I know what you meant by that. You think my wings should be spread all over your bed."

He laughed as he nodded. "And they should."

Shaking my head, I just couldn't figure out how to get through to the man. "I don't want to be that girl. The one who sleeps with her boss and has to find somewhere else to work, building her life up again after it all comes crashing down."

"You want promises that no one can give you, Ariel." He took me by the chin. "You don't know what will happen between us."

"But I do know what will happen between us if I don't give in," I said as I took a step back so his hand fell from my face, no longer sending sparks shooting all through me. "If I don't give in, then I will keep my job, my home, and my sanity."

Tilting his head to one side, his blue eyes sparkling with curiosity, he asked, "What is it that you don't want to give into, Ariel? Me, or the attraction you have for me?"

He'd hit the nail on the head, and I hated that. Throwing my hands in the air, I turned and walked back to my bungalow. "Ugh! How can I get through to you?"

The sound of him chuckling followed me to my door. "I'll be at the cantina if you decided to stop being so obstinate about things."

I didn't bother to look back at him. I just went inside and straight to my sofa where I plopped down and buried my head beneath the throw pillows. "He's so damn sexy and handsome and utterly exasperating!"

Sitting up, I ran my hand through my hair to smooth the unruly curls out somewhat. All around the island I saw couple after couple. No one seemed to be as worried about the consequences of their love affairs. No one else seemed concerned about having a place to be left alone to lick their wounds once their relationships were over. So why was I worried about what might happen? Why couldn't I be as carefree?

Had the death of my father and what happened afterward affected me so much? Had it broken me in a way that made me different from so many others?

If that was the truth, then Galen Dunne and I were more alike than I'd realized. He didn't believe in a love that could last forever, and maybe I didn't believe that either, at least subconsciously. If I was so worried about the possibility of things ending, then that meant I wasn't certain that things were set in stone.

The epiphany, rather than upsetting me, had me feeling exhilarated.

Nothing lasts forever.

I went to my room to freshen up. I was going to go get a drink with the man. I wasn't going to worry about the insane chemistry I felt with him, and I was going to throw away my idea that we had to have so much love between us that it would be guaranteed never to end. For if he could be truthful with himself about that, then I should be able to as well.

As I walked down the beach toward the cantina, I spotted Mr. Dunne sitting at the bar, talking to a man. I didn't want to bother him, so I kept on walking down the beach.

The more I walked, the more my confidence started to fade.

Maybe this was a bad idea after all.

I'd come out in bare feet, so I took a couple of steps over to walk in the surf. My head swam with doubts. What if I'm wrong? What if I'm making things up in my head just to get a taste of the man I've yearned for? What if I get hurt? What if he gets hurt? What if we both get hurt?

"Ariel?" Galen's deep voice rumbled by my ear just as he took hold of my shoulder. "Did you come for me?"

"I might've." We stopped and looked at each other for a moment.

"I've got a present for you." He took my hand, turning us back toward the bungalows. "It's at my place. Come on."

Without saying a word, I went with him, allowing myself to be in the moment and not think about what might happen in the future.

He took me inside, then picked up a pink bag from the desk in the living area. "I saw this in the gift shop this morning, and you came to mind."

Taking the bag, I looked inside to find a box. "What is it?" I lifted the box out of the bag and saw that it was a camera—a very expensive-looking camera. "Mr. Dunne? I can't..."

"You can." He took the box away from me and used a knife he'd pulled from his pocket to open it. "You take pictures with your phone all the time. I thought you should have this so you can take better pictures. Who knows, you may find a calling as a photographer."

I did love to take pictures. "You certainly pay lots of attention to what I do, Mr. Dunne."

He pulled the camera out of the box, then placed it on the countertop as we stood at the bar that separated the living room and kitchen. "I do pay lots of attention to you, Ariel. I think about you more than I think about anything else."

"You do?" He'd never hidden the fact that he was attracted to me —that he wanted me—but I didn't think it was something that took up that much of his time or thoughts.

"I do." One finger trailed along my jawline. "Your favorite food is a fresh salad with smoked turkey on top. The only dressing you'll use is olive oil and balsamic vinegar. You prefer water to any other drink. And I do believe that your favorite color is the same shade as your eyes—emerald. You see, I pay lots of attention to you. I find you fascinating, Ariel Pendragon."

I knew a thing or two about Mr. Dunne as well. I wouldn't have been standing there with him, alone in his home, if I hadn't. "You prefer red wine over white. But that's not your favorite drink—your favorite might surprise a lot of people. You like to drink milk more than anything else. Your go-to foods are those protein bars you have stashed everywhere. And I think your favorite color is the same as mine."

His knuckles grazed my cheek as he gazed into my eyes. "It is. As soon as I looked into these amazing eyes, it changed."

With a sigh, I gave in just a little. Easing into his warmth, I ran my hands up his arms then around his neck as I pulled my body closer to his. He stayed still, letting me come to him in my own time.

Our eyes held until our lips got so close that I could feel his warm breath flow over me. Then I touched mine to his, and the floor gave way beneath my feet.

Please don't let this be a mistake.

CHAPTER 12

Galen

Nothing had ever felt better than having Ariel in my arms—her lips pressed to mine, our bodies flush. Nothing else could compare to this feeling. And she'd kissed me this time. Ariel was losing the battle she'd waged within herself, and I couldn't have been happier.

I took in every aspect of her: the way her curls felt like satin between my fingers as I ran my hand through her hair; the way her hip bones jutted out, touching my stomach; the way her hands moved over my shoulders, stopping to rest on my biceps.

Her lips parted, allowing my tongue entrance to a place it had long missed. She didn't know it, but she was slowly wrapping me around her finger with each slight brush of her tongue against mine.

Although young and inexperienced, Ariel knew how to get to me. I didn't even understand it myself, but she knew—instinctively—how to push every button I had.

She ran one hand down to take hold of mine, which was inching down her back to take a handful of plump ass. Pulling it around between us, she held our hands against her chest. I could feel the beat of her heart as she held mine tightly to her.

She pulled her mouth away from mine and I groaned in protest. "Feel that?"

I nodded. "Yes. Your heart's pounding. So is mine." I pulled our clasped hands to my chest, which was beating just as hard.

Her smile, coy and sly, made my heart beat even faster. "Why do hearts pound when people kiss? When they touch?"

"Excitement," I answered. "Why else?"

She blinked her long lashes a few times. "Not love?"

Oh, this again.

"Ariel, don't..."

She placed one finger to my lips. "I have kissed a man before. I have even had sex before. My heart never beat like this before. Has yours?"

I'd done lots of things to make my heart beat as hard as this. But there was a tinge of something else going on, too. "Baby, can't we just go along and see what happens? Can't we leave the word love out of this? For now?"

She closed her eyes. I thought she was about to pull herself out of my arms, and I would do anything—short of making promises to the girl that I couldn't keep—to make her stay right where she was.

"If I tell you that we can leave that word out of things for now, then can you tell me that you will allow love to come into your heart if it knocks at the door?"

How was I supposed to answer her? I didn't think love made a difference—that it wouldn't last even it if did come around. How could I tell her that I avoided it at all costs? I didn't want to feel heart-break. I never had, and I hoped I never would.

"I can tell you this, and this is the God's honest truth, Ariel. You will never have to leave your job here, even if we don't work out. I mean that. I would never take any of this away from you. Your life here, it's yours to control." I thought that might help her.

But she only looked deep into my eyes, piercing my soul. "If you and I don't work out, I won't want to work here any longer. I won't want to see this handsome face anymore if I can't call it my own."

No one had ever had the nerve to say such a thing to me before. Ariel wanted to call me her own. I'd never allowed a woman to do that before. I might be willing to change things up a bit with her, though. But then again, that might be a terrible mistake.

"I've already told you that we can be exclusive." I thought I should make things crystal clear for her. "That said, that doesn't mean either of us own the other. Do you understand what I'm saying?"

"I believe you're saying that if one of us isn't feeling it any longer, then they're free to walk away unscathed." The way her lower lip pouted made me smile.

"Things are much simpler that way." I thought about what she'd said about not wanting to work at the resort if things didn't work out. "And if things go south for us, then I can find a place for you to work with one of my colleagues. How does that sound?"

"Terrible." Slowly, her hand moved up my arm until she placed her palm on my cheek. "Yours are the eyes I want to see whenever I open mine. Yours is the gaze I want to feel linger on my face. Yours are the hands I yearn to feel caressing every inch of my skin. Yours is the heart I want to reside in, and I want you to reside in mine. And I never want any of that to stop."

She'd gone and made me into a mere puddle of the man I'd been. "Those sound like wedding vows, Ariel Pendragon."

"In a way, they're not too different. I vow that I will work for us. Do you vow the same? Or is it too much to ask?" Her eyes glistened, never letting mine go.

I'd heard people talk of work when they spoke of their relationships. I didn't want to think of romance as work. Particularly because it wasn't supposed to be a chore. But Ariel wasn't talking about a simple romance—she was talking about a full-fledged relationship. A thing I wasn't ready for.

"You're much too sweet and innocent for me to tell you only what you want to hear." I thought that that alone should tell her that I wasn't ready to commit to more than something physical. I thought she'd already understood that.

She moved her hand off my face, her soft gaze lingering on my lips. "Your kiss promises me a good time in bed. Your touch promises me incredible chemistry. The way your heart beats promises me that you could let me in, but only if your mind allows that. All I want is the promise that you won't fight it if it comes—that you'll let this feeling take you to where it's meant to. You will let it take us wherever we're meant to be."

I wasn't one to give out promises. Not to anyone.

But I knew she wouldn't give us what we needed until I made her that promise. Would it be a lie to tell her what she wanted to hear? Or would it be exactly what she'd asked for, a genuine promise?

"And what if I don't ever feel love, Ariel?" I asked her as I took her hands, holding them between us. "Will that be the end of us?"

"I don't know." At least she wasn't going to lie, either. "All I'm asking is that you give it a chance to grow, just as I will. I don't love you right now, if that helps. I'm not a step ahead of you or anything like that. I just can't go into this with the idea that it's just sex and good times. I need more than that."

"You need love," I whispered as I thought about her demand.

She shook her head. "No. I need the promise that you won't swat it away if it comes to you. That's all. And if it never sprouts, then we will both know that, won't we?"

"And if it comes for one of us and not the other, then what?" I had to know. What if it was I who became enamored and she didn't? Then what?

With a shrug, she said, "I suppose we would have to give the other person the chance to see if it caught up to them or not. All I want is for that word, that feeling, not to be taken off the table and stuffed under the rug. That's all I'm saying."

It was better than telling me no. "You do realize this will be my first semi-relationship, right? I've never talked this much with anyone I've had sex with."

"Semi?" she looked disturbed by that word. "I don't want you to limit us that way. What we will have will be a relationship. There will be nothing semi about it."

For someone so young, she certainly took the reins easily. I had to laugh a bit. "When did this fearsome woman rise up in you, my sweet Ariel?"

A blush covered her cheeks. "When I found myself thinking about how hard it was going to be to stay out of your strong arms. You see, I've got to protect myself—and you, too, even if you don't realize it. I've got to be strong for both our sakes. Otherwise I'll just be like every other woman you'd had in your life. I will not be taken that same way."

"I can see that." The way she kept surprising me had me thinking I should definitely let her take the reins. She might lead us both to a place we'd be very happy in.

Or was it foolish of me to allow a young thing like her to lead the way to a place neither of us had ever been?

Something told me I should step up and take charge. "You're a bit young. You haven't been around as many blocks as I have. How about you just settle back and let me lead you? I promise you that I can make you very happy. At least for a while."

With a sigh, she slid out of my arms. "No, thank you." As she turned to walk out my house, I felt the earth shaking beneath me, then realized that it was my legs that shook.

Her shoulders sloped, her head down, she walked to the door, taking the knob in her small hand.

Before she could turn it, I moved up behind her, placing my hands on her narrow shoulders as I nuzzled her soft lavender-scented hair. "What the hell. Let's do things your way. What can it hurt to open myself up to new things? I promise to allow love in if it comes my way. I promise to work on this...relationship if need be. I promise to give all of myself to you."

She turned to face me with a smile. "And I promise to give you all of me, too."

I felt my heart beginning to pound away in my chest again. "Does this mean we can get to the good part now?"

"It does." And there it was—what I'd been waiting weeks to hear.

"You will not be sorry." Overwhelmed with joy, I picked her up and carried her bridal-style into my bedroom, where I set to work right away, making sure to fulfill the promise of making her very happy.

As I tossed her onto my bed, she squealed with delight. "We're really doing this, aren't we?"

"Strip." I began to undress.

She only shook her head. "I don't think so, sir."

"You're done with the sir shit," I informed her as I pushed my shorts down to the floor. "I am Galen."

"Okay, Galen." She leaned up on her elbows, eyeing me as I stood in front of her wearing only my tight, black boxer briefs. "Nice. Very nice. Now please tell me that you've got a wrapper in here."

"A wrapper?" I asked with confusion before it clicked. "Oh, a condom."

She nodded. "I'm not on any type of birth control. It wasn't the easiest thing to get, living out on the streets."

"Yes, I've got some in here." I watched her sexy smile as I went to the drawer that had a cache of them stuck behind the socks.

"I thought you might." Rolling over on her stomach, she watched me as I pulled one off the roll, then thought better of it and pulled off two more.

Only then did she begin unbuttoning her white shirt, her eyes on me the whole time.

I'm not sure what I've done, but I'm damn glad I've done it.

CHAPTER 13

Ariel

Skin to skin at last, Galen kissed me as he moved his body to cover mine. With weeks of anticipation behind us, it didn't take long for us to move to the main event. He knew I was more than ready. I spread my legs eagerly for him, and he eased down until the tip of his hard cock barely touched the outer rim of my sex.

The fire that raged inside me beckoned me to arch my back, pushing my sex up for him to enter. The tip of him went in, then he slowly moved deeper. A flurry of sensations flooded me all at once—desire, pleasure, fear, and eventually, pure bliss.

Raking my nails across his back, I moaned, "Galen, this feels amazing."

He leaned over me as he made smooth, even thrusts. "You feel incredible. Like nothing I've felt before." Galen raised his head, looking into my eyes. "I feel as if I've been waiting my whole life for this moment."

I prayed he would want more than just this one moment like this. I was very worried about how he would react after we made love the first time. Would he run? Be done with me already? Would his ego lash out at the control I demanded, turning him into someone I could never love?

Questions flooded my mind as we began to make love for the first time, until he did something that took me out of my own head completely. His hand moved through my hair and then he fisted a chunk, pulling it hard as he made a sudden change in his speed and intensity. "Fuck, baby, you're so tight!"

Galen was turning savage on me. At first I was afraid, gripping him by his arms to hold myself in place as he moved with such force that I was being pushed further up the bed. "Galen!" I gasped.

He moved one arm underneath my knee, jerking it up until my knee was next to my ear. I could feel myself stretching as the new angle let him go even deeper. "Say it again, baby."

"Galen," I moaned as his cock filled me entirely. "Oh, God, Galen."

The lingering fear now replaced by pure lust, my head was light, my mind on nothing but the sensation of our bodies colliding. This wasn't at all like what I'd experienced before. What I'd done with my first lover didn't seem like sex at all compared to what Galen was doing to my body.

My legs began to tremble, and Galen moved his arm, releasing my leg before he pulled out of me entirely, leaving me shaking and confused. He grinned at me as he took in my confused expression. "On your knees."

Moving to get up on my knees, I found him laughing as I stood up on my knees. "What?"

He ran one hand over his face. "Hands and knees, baby."

"Oh, doggy-style. I get it now." I felt like a rookie. But then again, I was. I assumed the position then gasped again as he pushed my back until my chest and head were on the mattress. I felt vulnerable, splayed out with my ass in the air. "Galen?"

Slam!

He thrust into me so hard that it rocked my entire body. His hand connected with my bottom with a loud smack and I shouted with surprise, "Galen!"

His voice had gone harsh and rugged, "Say it again. Say my name."

"Galen!" I shrieked as he slammed into me harder and harder, giving my butt smack after smack. And then the shaking began again, and this time it was accompanied by a wave of pure pleasure that came from deep inside of me. "Galen," I moaned with desire. "Oh, Galen, take me. Take me, baby. Take me all the way." My words turned into a howling moan as my body crested and I had my first ever orgasm.

I'd thought I'd had orgasms before—I was no stranger to masturbation. But those sensations were nothing compared to this; those had been the mere edge of climaxing. Galen took me all the way there and kept me there for quite some time.

His deep laugh filled my ears as my whole body pulsed, and my sex grew so wet it didn't seem possible. "Give it to me, baby."

I could barely breathe as he pulled out of me, and I fell to the bed. But then he took me by the shoulder to roll me onto my back. Pulling my weak knees up, he moved in between my legs, settling back inside of me with a sexy grin on his handsome face.

Cradling his face between my hands, I looked into his piercing blue eyes. "It seems you have a talent."

"I know." He kissed me softly, then pulled back to look at me as he started slowly stroking inside of me again. "You make me wilder than anyone ever has. I think I can do this all night long. What do you think?"

I never wanted to stop feeling this way—these intense sensations and emotions. "Count me in."

One finger trailed over my collar bone, then down between my breasts. "Mind if I have a taste?"

I'd never had my tits sucked before. And honestly, I didn't think it would be something I would like. "I don't know."

"If you hate it, then just tell me to stop." He always knew just what to say to get me to say yes.

I watched him as he put his hot mouth on my left breast. When his lips touched the tip of my nipple, ripples of adrenaline moved through me. His tongue ran over the tip, making it even harder. I could feel it growing bigger with arousal.

I ran my hands through his thick dark hair as he began to suck gently. "Ah, Lord, this is good." Everything he did felt better than I'd ever expected.

As he sucked, he kept moving with slow motions until my body was on fire once more, and I had no choice but to give into another orgasm.

My body shook once again, and then he lifted his head up to look at me as I came undone beneath him. "God, you're even more gorgeous when you come, Ariel. I want to keep you coming all night long."

My chest heaved as I tried to catch my breath, while he hardly seemed winded. "How are you able to hold back so easily?" I had to ask. So far, there had been a severe inequality when it came to orgasms.

"It's not easy at all." He kissed the tip of my nose. "Your cunt is so tight. And when you orgasm, it clenches all around my hard cock, making me want to give in. But giving into my needs isn't part of my mission. My mission is to make you want more of me. I want to show you what I can do for you, Ariel. I want to make you crave this. Crave sex."

"Should that be a thing?" I asked. "To crave sex?"

"Well, in this situation, yes." He took my lips softly at first, and then he took the kiss to a hard place, a demanding place.

Moving his tongue deeper and deeper into my mouth, I soon found him stroking the back of my tongue with his own. He pushed his cock inside me at the same pace he moved his tongue, and finally, I understood what he was doing. He was showing me a glimpse of how it would feel to suck him off.

My nails gouged into the flesh of his back, finding it so exciting that he wanted me to do that to him. As incompetent as I was, he trusted me to take his organ into my mouth and do the right thing with it.

Galen would push me to my limits; I knew that now. He would teach me all he knew, and I hoped I could teach him some things, too. Like how to let go of it all and give oneself to another.

Not that I knew how to do that, either, since I'd never done it before. But it was something that I felt deep in my soul could be done. At that moment I knew I didn't want to do this with anyone but Galen Dunne. And I didn't want him to do this with anyone else, either.

Running my foot up the back of his leg, I moaned as he made a little grinding motion with his pelvis. He did that a few more times, and my clit pulsed as another wave of pleasure rolled inside of me.

This orgasm was deep, and this time he couldn't help himself as my body had taken its toll on his. Pulling his mouth away from mine, he panted and growled, making such deep, guttural sounds that they shook his body as he came.

The condom stopped me from feeling the rush of his hot seed as it spurted from him. I felt disappointed at that, like I was missing something. Our bodies had been almost like one until then. Only then did it feel as if I'd been denied something.

Once he'd stopped groaning, he opened his eyes to look down at me. "You okay?"

I nodded. "Are you?" I ran my hands through his hair. "That was some noise you made there."

"You brought the animal out in me." He kissed my cheek. "I've gotta get off you now for a bit. I've gotta get rid of this rubber."

I felt suddenly alone as he moved off me. He walked away to the lavatory to clean himself up. When he came back, he had a cloth in his hand and handed it to me. "I suppose you want me to clean myself up."

"If you'd like. I know I didn't get my stuff all over you, but we managed to get you quite wet." He said with a wink before heading out of the room. He stopped walking away to turn back to look at me. "I'm getting us some water. And I've got to know something."

"What?" I had no idea what he wanted to know, but I was sure it was related to sex.

"Had you ever had a real orgasm before that?" He eyed me, seeing if I would lie, I supposed.

"I've given myself some before." I had to admit that he'd done a much better job at that than I'd ever managed, though. "But none ever felt as good as the ones you've given me. Those were real gifts, I must say."

The smile that moved over his lips made my heart race. "Good. I'll be right back. I'm not anywhere near finished with you, baby."

Giving myself a good squeeze, I was glad to hear that he wasn't ready for this night to end.

This seems a little too good to be true. But I hope it never ends.

CHAPTER 14

Galen

Three glorious months passed with me and Ariel spending our nights together as well as our days. I'd stayed on longer at the island than I had the previous years. The weather on the island remained the same as always, warm with clear skies and tons of sun.

Back in Portland, Oregon, where I'd purchased an estate for my parents to live, the weather had turned cool as autumn had set in. A call from my mother on Thanksgiving Day had me smiling as I answered my phone. "Ma, it's so good to hear from you. How is this Thanksgiving Day treating ya?"

My family had eagerly started celebrating the North American holiday as soon as they'd relocated to the States, and I was a sucker for it as well.

"Very well. The cook has made all the usual delicious dishes. All the family is coming over to join us. You'll be missed, Galen. And I will expect you to be here for Christmas, son. You won't miss out on every holiday this year." My mother made sure our family got together on most holidays, but I wasn't always able to make it. Christmas was the one time when she demanded attendance.

"I'll be there. I'm not about to provoke your wrath." I laughed as I thought about my five-foot-tall mother shaking her tiny fist at me as she ranted and raved about how no one is ever too busy to spend time with family.

"Give us a week, will you?" she asked.

That, I didn't know about. If Ariel agreed to go with me to Portland, then I'd maybe consider it. If not, then I wouldn't stay more than a night. Ariel had become someone I depended on. Sleeping without her would be pure hell. Why put myself through hell?

"I'll see about that, Ma." I wasn't about to go making false promises.

"See that ya do, Mr. Dunne," her tone was sharp. "I'll not be bartered with. I think ya know that, son. I want a week of my oldest son's time. That's not too much to ask for—especially since I haven't had a day of your presence all year."

She was right. I had to give her and the rest of my family at least a week of my time. "I'll be there, Ma. And I might be bringing a special friend of mine home with me this year."

"A special friend?" I'd piqued her interest. "A girl, finally?"

"You'll have to wait to see about that." I loved surprising her. "I'll be letting you know when I'm coming in next month. You enjoy your Thanksgiving feast. Love to you and the rest of the family. Bye now."

"Love to you, too, Galen. Goodbye."

With the call over, I left my bungalow to go to Ariel's. She'd gotten into the spirit of celebrating her first Thanksgiving—many of the guests and employees on the island were American, so everyone had been abuzz the past few weeks—and she'd decided to prepare our first Thanksgiving dinner herself. I was happy to comply, loving the thought of her going to this effort for us to share a special meal together.

But as I came through her door, I was ambushed by a cloud of smoke and the sound of her huffing and puffing.

The aroma of burnt everything hung in the air. "Ah, this seems like a great time to tell you that there's a buffet going on at The Royal today."

Her auburn hair was braided, but a bit had come unraveled, and it hung in her face. She blew the loose strands out of the way. "Galen, I wanted to do this for you so badly. But everything is either burnt or raw."

Taking her by the shoulders, I directed her to her bedroom. "Go shower and change into something nice. I'll clean this up while you get ready to go out for our Thanksgiving meal."

"It's a real mess, Galen. Don't bother. I'll tackle it when we get back. I'm so sorry about this." She shook her head as I pushed her along.

"You just do as I've said." I got her into her room, closed the door behind her, then set to work cleaning up the mess she'd made.

Poor thing, she'd done it all for me anyway. The least I could do was clean up her attempt at making a memorable meal.

An hour later, she emerged just as I'd finished wiping down the countertops. "Galen!" Her hands flew to her hips. "I told you not to clean up."

"Well, I felt like doing it, so I did. Sue me." I went to her, wrapping my arm around her waist. "Come, let us enjoy this meal. I've got a question to ask you, too."

"And that question is?" She looked at me with wide eyes.

"It's been three months since we've started seeing each other." I felt I should start the conversation with the timeline for our budding relationship. It might be crucial to her answer.

"Yes, it's been a short time." I didn't like how she'd put it.

"And in that amount of time, we've learned a lot about each other. Both good and bad." Our living habits hadn't always meshed, and that largely accounted for the 'bad' I referenced. She didn't like to do her bathroom business with me around, so she'd go to her place every morning after we got up. It was a thing we'd argued about a few times.

"Yes, we have." She and I left her bungalow to go to the restaurant. "But we're still on the same shaky terms we were when we started this, so I would say that we've got a ways to go before we know if this is going anywhere or not."

I didn't much like the sound of that. "Where does this need to go, Ariel?" If she was looking for a proposal, I wasn't nearly ready for that.

"I don't want to get into it," she replied. "I'm a little frazzled from my disaster. Can't we drink some wine and eat some good food and just let today take us wherever it will?"

"Fine with me." I pulled her closer to my side, resolving to do as she said and drop it for now. "As long as I've got you by my side, I can be thankful for anything." I kissed the side of her head, making her laugh.

Her hand moved to rest on my chest as she gazed at me. "You make me happy."

"You do the same for me." I kissed her lips softly, and we kept walking toward the restaurant.

There were no guests and only a skeleton crew of staff on the island. Everyone else had gone home for the holiday break. I gave everyone who wanted it two months off to enjoy both Thanksgiving and Christmas.

Being that Ariel had nowhere else to go, I wasn't about to leave her alone while I went away. She'd become very special to me. So special that I found myself wondering if she were someone I could ever live without.

But even feeling that way, I wasn't ready to make any significant commitments. We were taking things nice and slow. Both of us were happy with that.

The smell of roasted turkey hit me as we came through the glass doors. "Ah, now this is what Thanksgiving smells like, my darling."

"Maybe I'll get it right next year," she said with a frown. "This smells wonderful. Not once did my kitchen smell this way. Not even once." Her little pout was adorable, and I quickly dropped a kiss on her lips.

The maintenance man and his wife sat at one table. They waved as we came in and went to the buffet. Bottles of wine had already been opened and left to breathe, and I took one then placed it on a nearby table. "I've got the drink covered."

Ariel was piling the food on her plate. "This looks so yummy."

I liked how the woman ate. She wasn't afraid of food the way a lot of women I'd been with were. Ariel wasn't skin and bones at all, nor was she obese. Pleasantly plump in all the right places—that's how I would describe her.

Making my own plate, I joined her at the table for two where she waited for me. When she reached for my hand, I took it. "Does this mean you want me to say a prayer over our meal?"

She nodded. "My father used to say a prayer when I was young. Would you do that today, since this is a special meal?"

I had to admit that I'd never been one for prayer since I made it to adulthood. I'd left those traditions with my childhood. But her asking me to do something her father had done made my heart fill with joy. "I will."

We bowed our heads and closed our eyes. I said a little prayer then we opened our eyes and looked at each other. She smiled so prettily at me. "Thank you, Galen. That was very nice."

"Shall we dig in now?" I asked as I pulled my eyes off her to look at the overflowing plate before me.

"We shall." She laughed as she stabbed a piece of turkey. "I'm so hungry! I'm going to be stuffed after this."

"Stuff away, baby. We'll take a nice long nap later." I put a forkful of green bean casserole into my mouth.

We said little as we ate, then we waddled back to my bungalow, plopping down on the sofa, both of us sighing as we fell. The doors to the patio were open, letting in the warm air and allowing us to look out at the evening sky over the rippling water.

Laying my head back on the sofa, I turned to look at her. She'd already dropped her head back, too. "I want you to come to my parents' place with me for Christmas."

"In Portland? You want to take me to the estate you bought them?" she asked without a hint of a smile on her pretty face. I found that to be a little on the alarming side.

"Yes, and I've got a whole wing there. We'd have lots of privacy." I didn't want her to think it would be like we had to sleep on a fold-out couch or anything like that.

"I don't know, Galen." She looked away from me, her eyes going to the ceiling. "It's only been three months. I don't know if that's what people do when they've only been seeing each other for that short of a time."

"First of all, it's been three months of nights and days together. That's a lot of time to spend with a person. And it doesn't matter what other people do." I could see I was going to have to do some convincing if I wanted her to come with me. "And I've already told my mother that I might be bringing a special person home for the holiday."

She turned her face to look at me again. "Special?"

I reached out to run my knuckles across her pink cheek. "You are special to me, Arial Pendragon."

"Special enough to get you to say I was more than just special?" She grinned. "Like, would you call me your girlfriend?"

I'd never called anyone my girlfriend. I wasn't particularly a fan of that term. "Special is a good thing to be called. Don't you think?"

"It's nice enough." She looked up again. "But if you called me your girlfriend, then it would be even nicer. It would mean more, if you and I are boyfriend and girlfriend. Not merely special friends. Do you understand what I'm saying?"

"Do you understand that I am over forty and the thought of being called anyone's boyfriend sounds ridiculous to me?" I could see how someone her age would get a kick out of that, but I wasn't so sure that anyone my age would.

"I guess I could call you my manfriend." She grinned. "Nah, that sounds even sillier."

"Let's just stick with special friends for now. What do you say to that?" I asked, then added, "And to going with me for Christmas?"

"You've left me with little choice, haven't you?" She winked at me. "I suppose it would be rather lonely without you here during Christmas."

I took her hand, rubbing my thumb over the back of it. "It would be very lonely without me here."

"And you might miss me if you were away, too," she mused.

"I would most definitely miss you." I knew I would.

She arched one brow. "Is your mother one of those people who expects a lot out of the women you bring home?"

"I have no idea." It wasn't a lie. "I've never brought any woman to meet my family before."

The way her eyes lit up made my heart dance. "Well, then, by all means, my answer is yes. A thousand times yes."

Those were the best words I'd heard in a very long time.

CHAPTER 15

Ariel

"I've never met anyone's parents before." I twisted my hands in my lap nervously as we pulled through the enormous iron gate that led to his parent's estate. "Is it normal to be this nervous, Galen?"

"I have no idea." He ran his arm around my shoulders as his parents' driver drove us up to the mansion he'd bought for his parents a few years back. "I'm not nervous at all. I know they'll adore you. You're easily adored, you know. Adorable. Haven't I called you that before?"

He'd called me that once. When I was sitting on the toilet, and he'd come in without knocking. I'd shaken my fist at him and threatened to knock him out if he didn't stop smiling and leave at once.

Galen had this weird idea that being in the lavatory at the same time wasn't a big deal at all. He often said to me that we took showers together, so what did doing anything else in there matter? Well, I thought the other things I did in there were no one's business but my own, and I planned on keeping it that way.

"You have, but it doesn't lessen my nerves." I grabbed his hand as we pulled to a stop at the front entrance, which was so impressive I thought we'd stopped in front of a grand hotel rather than a home. "Galen, this is beyond gorgeous."

"I think so, too." He slid out once the driver opened the door. The fact that he had my hand in his gave me no other option than to go along with him, although I'd have rather kept my bottom firmly planted on the Italian leather seat of the limousine.

"Galen, maybe this is too soon." I clung to him as if he was a life preserver, and we'd fallen into stormy seas.

"There's nothing to worry about, my darling girl." He wrapped his arm around my shoulders, kissing me on the cheek.

I had a little more on my mind than just the meeting of his family. Mother Nature had seen fit to delay my monthly visitor by two weeks. I'd never been the most regular, and we'd never had sex without a condom, but I also knew that condoms were not one hundred percent effective. And I also knew that there had been a few times when things had seemed a little extra slippery. ...and there'd been a few times when we'd been a little reckless.

I had to admit that I was to blame for our recklessness. I'd wanted Galen to show me what it felt like to have his bare cock inside of me, so we made love for a while without the condom on. After a while, as he got closer to letting go, he put the condom on. We both liked the sensations so much that we'd done it a couple times. Since those adventures, I'd read up a bit on the subject and found more than one couple had found themselves pregnant by following the same idea.

I was already nervous about meeting his family, and the thought of doing so with a bun in the oven—one Galen knew nothing about —would have been near unbearable. So I hadn't taken a pregnancy test as of yet. I wanted to give Mother Nature a little longer of a chance to kick in before then.

"My mother cannot wait to meet you, Ariel. Please give her a warm response. She's been on pins and needles over the fact I'm finally bringing a woman home to meet her," Galen's words only served to make my nerves even worse.

Butterflies swarmed my tummy as the door opened, and a

doorman stood there with a stoic look in his pale blue eyes. "Mr. Dunne. What a pleasure it is to see you again. Your mother and father have been waiting as patiently as possible for you and your special friend to arrive."

Galen wasted no time on introductions. "This is Miss Ariel Pendragon, James. She's my special friend."

The tall older man nodded at me. "A pleasure, Miss Pendragon." He took a step back to allow us inside. "If you will follow me, I will take you to the solarium."

Following along behind the man, I whispered to Galen, "What's a solarium?"

He whispered back, "A room with lots of windows, including in the ceiling. My mother likes to keep lots of plants, and she loves to hang out in there."

So, she had a green thumb. I finally had a starting point for what to do for a gift. I'd plied Galen for ideas, but he'd told me not to worry about it. He'd already had his personal assistant take care of the presents he would give his family, and my name had been added to all the tags right next to his.

Galen's thoughtfulness proved to me that he cared more for me than he had in the beginning. Our relationship had grown, and our feelings had as well. I just hoped none of that would end if I were pregnant.

I had no idea how Galen would take such news. But I knew there wasn't any other option for me. I would keep our baby, whether he wanted to be a father or not.

Though I'd been freaked out by the mere possibility at first, the longer my period stayed away, the more I grew fond of the idea.

Going through room after room, we finally came to the one his parents were in. His mother looked nothing like I thought she would. I'd pictured a woman with dark curls much like her son's. Her arms wide open, she greeted us loudly. "He's finally here! Our eldest is home, Johnathon."

Even as she hugged Galen, she looked at me with light green eyes, her red hair up in a bun. I smiled at her shyly and gave a little wave. Another boisterous voice called out from behind me, "And you must be Miss Ariel Pendragon of the London Pendragons."

I turned to find a tall man with white hair towering over me. "And you must be Mr. Dunne."

His arms enveloped me, nearly crushing me to his chest. "John, my dear. Just John."

I responded as soon as he let me go, finally being able to catch my breath. "It's a pleasure to meet you, John."

My hand was taken, and Galen turned me back to his mother. "Ariel, this is my mother, Felicity Dunne."

I extended my hand. "It's a pleasure to meet you, ma'am." I didn't know what to call her and dared not call her by her first name.

She cocked one brow. "Ma'am? No, no—I am Felicity. And may I call you Ariel?"

"Of course! I'll have it no other way." When she opened her arms invitingly, I moved into them, hugging her.

"Glad to hear that, dear." Galen's mother smelled of roses and peppermint, an endearing scent that left me missing my own mother. When she let me out of her grasp, she patted the top of my hand, which she hadn't let go of. "Galen has told us of your mother's unfortunate passing not too long ago. And your father's before that. I hope you won't mind if we treat you like family, dear."

My heart swelled. "That would be very nice. And might I do the same?"

John's hand rested on my shoulder, making me turn to look at him. "We will have it no other way, my darling girl."

Galen couldn't have looked one bit happier than he did as I stood between his parents. "This is starting off well. How about some Scotch?"

I didn't think I should drink any alcohol until I knew whether I was pregnant or not. "I'd love a soda. The jet ride gave me a bit of jetlag. I wouldn't want to aggravate that with alcohol."

Felicity smiled at me. "I'll have soda, too. Leave the Scotch to the gentlemen." She looped her arm through mine, pulling me away from Galen and his father and keeping me to herself for a while. "Do you enjoy the company of plants, Ariel?"

"I've never known any." I looked at a plant with long pink fronds hanging from it. "But your collection is extraordinary. These aren't all native to America, are they?"

"Not by far." She took me to sit on a wicker loveseat with a flowery cushion. It creaked under our combined weight, but I found it stable once we sat. "I have plants here from the Middle East all the way to Australia."

I knew I'd have to do my research if I was to get her anything she didn't already have. "My, that's quite the distance."

"And I love to travel to pick up my gems." Well, she'd gone and taken that option off the gift list.

Back to zero.

I'd never had the money to buy anyone any type of present before. It had been one of those things I'd thought I would enjoy doing—until I found myself spending Christmas with the family of a billionaire.

Perhaps personal baked goods.

Who was I kidding? I was a disaster in the kitchen.

Maybe I would have to settle with being on the tag with Galen after all.

"It's nice to get to meet the people who raised the remarkable Galen Dunne. Tell me, was he precocious as a child?" I had the feeling he had to have been.

"Galen was three before he said a single word." She tapped her chin as she looked at him standing a ways from us, talking to his father. "After his first word, he learned pretty quickly. It wasn't long before we heard a full sentence from him. I'll never forget it," she said with a motherly smile. "He'd said, 'Ma, can I have a cake?' And I asked him, 'You want a whole cake? To yourself?' He'd nodded, and so I made him a cake. I made it smaller than most, but he still ate every last bit of that cake. He even said thank you afterwards."

I didn't know what to say to a story like that. "That's not usual for a child that age, is it?"

"None of the rest of my children ever did a thing like that." A maid came by wearing a black and white maid uniform and offered up our sodas on a tray. Felicity took one and handed it to me, then took the other. "Thank you, Sharon. By the way, this is Ariel. She'll be staying the holiday with us. She's Galen's special friend."

The maid's eyes cut to me, then to the floor. "It's a pleasure, Ariel. Let me know if you need anything."

"Nice to meet you, Sharon. I'll be sure to let you know if I need anything." I thought I'd warn her that we might not need to take her up on her services. "I'm Galen's personal maid, so I'm used to seeing to myself and him."

The young woman's eyes grew wide. "You are his maid? Even now?"

I nodded. "I am."

The way Galen's mother frowned made me wonder if I'd said something I should've kept to myself. "You're still his maid, Ariel?"

"I am." I looked at her with worry. "Is that a problem?"

"It should be for you." She looked at Sharon, who then scurried away. "Aren't you and he—um. Well, aren't you and he having relations?"

I was speechless at the question; I never would've imagined I'd be discussing sex with Galen's mom within moments of meeting her. But the truth seemed right. "We are."

"And he pays you?" She shook her head in disagreement.

"Not for that," I clarified.

"No, you shouldn't be working for him in that regard any longer." She wasn't okay with me being paid by him in any capacity—that was plain.

"Felicity, I need to have my independence. I don't want to live off anyone. I want to make my own money. And neither Galen nor I want me to be his maid—or anyone else's—forever. He gave me a camera a little while back, and I've begun taking lots of pictures to hone my skills. I think I might like to be a photographer. Once I can make money doing that, I'll end the maid job with him." At least that was a plan I'd loosely made.

"Good." She patted the back of my hand. "I just don't think you should tell everyone that little bit about the job. It sounds a bit off, if you know what I mean."

CHAPTER 16

Galen

Ariel's auburn hair was splayed over the white linen pillowcase, and it looked too inviting not to run my fingers through. "You've never looked lovelier."

Ariel looked up at me with no smile on her face. "Do you think they really like me, Galen? Or are they only being nice?"

"They like you, silly girl." I leaned down to place a kiss on her pink lips. "Who wouldn't like you? You're wonderful."

"They are, too." I'd spent three days with his parents, and I'd enjoyed every minute of it. "Tomorrow is Christmas Eve though, and the rest of your family is coming. Do you think your younger sisters and your brother will like me, too?"

"No," I teased her. I thought better of it as her lower lip stuck out in a pout. I kissed her once more. "I'm joking. Of course they'll like you. My family is very easy to get along with. Now, I will warn you that Becca will expect you to share a pint with her if she's to trust ya."

Panic filled her green eyes. "A pint of beer?"

I had to laugh. "Why the panicked look?" It wasn't as if she'd never had a pint or two.

"I just don't feel like drinking alcohol." She ran her hand over her stomach. "My nerves haven't been so great, dealing with meeting your family. I think alcohol would only serve to aggravate them."

"Or it might alleviate them altogether." I ran my hand over her bare belly that was on display, both of us having shed our clothes long ago. "It won't hurt to have a pint with her if she offers ya one."

Nodding, she gulped. "Sure. Okay." Her hands ran up my arms then she cupped my face. "I noticed that your mother is quite a bit younger than your father."

"True. He's seventeen years older than she is. They met when she was only a teen in high school. Fifteen, I think."

Ariel smiled. "And her hair is red, and her eyes are green. Galen, do I remind you of your mother?"

I'd never noticed that before. "Is that weird?"

She shook her head, making her auburn curls dance on the pillowcase. "I don't think it's weird at all. I think it means more than you know."

I thought it might mean more, too. "Like why I think you're so special?'

She nodded. "The reason you look at me with such emotion in your blue eyes."

Perhaps she was right. I had no idea why only Ariel had managed to make me feel so many things that no one else ever had. But I did know one thing: I was about to change things up.

My mother had brought up the idea of going to our home in Ireland in the spring when the weather was at its best. She'd taken it upon herself to invite Ariel along, and when Ariel had looked at me with diamonds in her eyes, I knew she wanted to go more than anything.

I'd told her then that we would see and give my mother an answer later in the coming year. Ariel's sparkle had faded. I hated the feeling that had come over me when I saw that look on her face. But I didn't want Ariel and my mother making all sorts of plans if they couldn't be seen through. Especially if my mother was true to her nature and began making purchases and prepaid plans.

I trailed my fingers along her long throat. "Your beauty—inside and out—makes me look at you with so much emotion. I never thought I would be able to look at someone and feel my heart racing. At times, I find it a bit scary, to be honest with you."

Ariel's expression grew curious. "Was your father married before he married your mother?"

"No. She was his one and only wife." I had no idea what she was getting at.

"So, the Dunne men take a little longer to find the women that are meant for them, huh?" She smiled at me as her nails grazed my back.

"Oh, you think I've found the woman for me then, do ya?" I tickled her, making her laugh.

"Stop! You're gonna make me wet myself. Stop!" Her laughter made me feel lighter than air.

Settling in next to her, I pulled the blanket up to my chin. "Ariel, we've been taking things slow, and I really like that about us."

She turned to her side then lay her head on my chest. "I'm not trying to rush you, Galen. It's never been my intention to do that. I hope you know that."

Drawing her hand up to my lips, I nibbled on it, then kissed her palm. "I know, you've never done anything to rush this. And I'm glad for that." I kissed a trail along her arm then got an idea and pulled the blanket over my head as I pushed her to lie back on the bed.

"Uh oh," she said quietly. "Are you about to rock my world?"

I didn't answer her as I kissed my way down her stomach, then moved her legs to allow me to kiss her sweet pearl. The way it pulsed against my lips made my cock hard. Nothing tasted sweeter to me than her nectar.

Running my tongue through her warm folds, I let myself go, making her pleasure my only concern. My hands moved to grip her plump ass, lifting her up so I could kiss her more deeply.

Her soft flesh squished in my hands as I massaged and caressed her fine ass. Ariel had a great pair of tits and an ass that refused to quit. I'd been lucky to woo her into my bed.

Sex with Ariel had surpassed any ideas I'd had before. Sex and good times were plentiful for us. She'd given me exactly what I'd needed from her. I couldn't have been more pleased.

Her little hole felt tight even around my tongue as I moved it inside of her. She wiggled and moaned softly as I licked her up and down then pushed my tongue into her. The sounds she made never failed to turn me on.

Even when we weren't in the bedroom, the right sound from her could get me hard in an instant. One afternoon on the island she'd been in the kitchen after sweeping and mopping the floor. The way she groaned when she picked up the heavy bucket of water sent my dick into rock-hard status immediately.

As she'd leaned over the edge of the deck to throw the dirty water away, I took advantage of her ass being up in the air and pulled her dress up. I'd ripped those panties right off before I took her on that deck.

I'd fucked her so hard that I had forgotten that I hadn't put on a condom. But I managed to jerk it out of her, spilling myself on the deck rather than inside her tight walls.

I was determined to get her to see a doctor before we left Portland to get her ass on the pill. And thereafter, the island doctor could keep her in birth control pills.

I craved the feel of her without the rubber between us. I'd never craved such a thing in my life. Ariel brought out new things in me all the time.

When her hands took hold of my head and her cries got louder, I knew she was about to give me what I wanted. Sweet fluid gushed from her, and I lapped it up, making sure to leave plenty to allow my cock a slick entrance.

Moving up her body, I thrust my hard-on into her still quivering channel as she looked at me. "Maybe going in without a condom is asking for trouble, babe. Maybe you should put one on."

"I'm taking care of that, baby." I kissed her lips then pushed my tongue into her mouth. "Taste that. That's all you."

I moved with a slow thrust, letting my cock take in the way she felt as I moved up and down, in and out, over and over again. Her nails dug into my arms as I kept going and going.

"Galen! Galen, oh God, don't stop," she moaned as she writhed beneath me.

Another orgasm was about to erupt within her, and I wanted to ride it out without the condom. "Do it, baby. Come all over my hard cock."

Her eyes opened, the emerald of them catching the light behind me. "But what if you can't stop yourself?"

I was panting with desire, but I knew I could control myself. "Don't worry about me. Get off on me, baby. I want to feel your hot juices coating my cock." It wasn't that dangerous of a game I played. I hadn't gone off inside of her yet. Neither of us was looking to start a family, not when we had no idea about our future.

"Only if you're sure," she moaned as she arched up to me.

"I'm sure." I was getting closer and closer. "Hurry." I was too close. "I'll just pull out before I come. Go for it."

The way her moans rose, I knew she was about to let loose, and I wasn't disappointed. Her tunnel clamped down on my cock hard, heat surrounding it. I was gasping, trying to keep myself controlled as her body pulled at mine, coaxing me to give it all I had to give.

She wrapped her legs around my waist, pulling me to her, not letting me go as she came over and over. "God! I can't stop!"

I needed her to let me go. "Baby, unwrap your legs."

She seemed almost reluctant to move her legs off me so I could pull out and let my release happen. "Shit!" She finally removed her legs and I quickly pulled out before spilling myself all over her stomach.

Huffing and puffing, she and I looked at each other as I fell on the bed beside her. "We've got to get you to a doctor. We've got to get you on the pill."

She got up, heading to the bathroom to clean herself up, no doubt. "I suppose a baby would be unwelcome."

I didn't say a word. I didn't think I had to. And by midnight the next night she would understand why I hadn't said a thing just then.

When she came back, she tossed me a damp cloth.

"Thanks. I am tuckered out after that," I said.

"I bet you are. That took some willpower right there." She climbed into bed, then turned over, facing away from me.

After cleaning up, I took my place at her back, spooning her from behind. Kissing her neck the way I'd become accustomed to, I felt the urge to tell her more than what I normally did. Somehow I resisted. "Goodnight, my darling."

"Goodnight, babe. See you in the morning." She pulled up my hand that was cupping her tit to give it a kiss. "It's going to be a big day tomorrow. I need to look my best."

"No need to worry about that. You always look beautiful no matter what." I hugged her to give her more confidence.

I had no worries at all about what the rest of my family would think of her. Not that I really cared, but I knew they'd all like her just the way she was—just as I did.

CHAPTER 17

Ariel

A bit after breakfast the next morning—Christmas Eve—I dashed out to visit the pharmacy. I'd seen one not too far from the estate and knew I could make the walk and no one would be the wiser.

Galen was busy helping his father hang stockings for all the grandchildren. Galen's brother had two boys, and his three sisters had twelve children altogether, so the mansion, although large—well, huge, actually—would soon be brimming with people. I'd taken advantage of everyone's busy morning to sneak out.

The air was cold, and snowflakes blew around me in wisps. The sky was gray, the sun nowhere to be seen. An ominous feeling had come over me, and I didn't know what it meant exactly. But I knew it came from the fear of change and what Galen and I would do if I were pregnant with his baby.

I had to know though—I couldn't wait until we left his parents' place. And if the results proved positive, then I would tell Galen about the baby right away. If they came out negative, then I wouldn't mention it at all. Either way, today would be a monumental day in my life.

Pulling my coat tighter around me to shut out the cold, I hurried to get to the corner. Across the street, the pharmacy's sign was lit in red letters. Ben's Pharmaceuticals. I would always remember that name, whether pregnant or not.

My tummy was rumbling with nerves, so I picked up a lemon-lime soda from the beverage display, then went to find just the right pregnancy test. Since I wasn't months past due, I had to find one that would give me early results. Thankfully, I found that most every one of them would work for me. My hand shook as I placed my purchases on the counter. An older woman rang up the goods, taking care to put the test in a brown paper bag so no one would see the contents. She gave me a conspiratorial look. "I suppose you don't want anyone to see that."

"You're right. It's a secret." I picked up the soda before she could put it in a bag. "I'll be drinking this on the walk back."

With a nod, she said, "Have a Merry Christmas."

"You, too." I left the store through the automatic sliding glass doors then popped the top on my soda, gulping it down and wishing it was something stronger.

My chest felt tight, my heart felt heavy, and my mind was full. Hurrying across the street, I saw the Dunne's limousine three cars back and knew some members of Galen's family were about to catch me walking up the road. I prayed the driver wouldn't recognize me and stop to offer a ride.

Pulling the hood of my coat up, I concealed my identity and hurried along. The last thing I needed was an introduction to anyone in Galen's family as I carried a pregnancy test back to their family home.

The car passed without even slowing down, and I breathed a sigh of relief as I trudged on. The snow began to thicken, and by the time I arrived at the back door of the mansion, it had become so thick I could barely see a foot in front of me.

The cooks were busy in the kitchen as I walked in. No one seemed to notice me, and I was grateful for that fact as I took the seldom used back staircase to head to Galen's wing.

I'd stuffed the bag with the test into my pocket and was thankful for that when Galen caught me just as I topped the stairs. "There you are. I've been looking everywhere for you." He looked at my coat, which I hadn't taken off yet. "You were outside? In this weather? Have you gone insane?"

"I wanted to walk around in the snow. What's insane about that?" I moved past him to get to his bedroom. "I'll just be a minute. Let me get this coat off. Why were you looking for me?"

"My brother and his family have arrived. I want to introduce you." He came up beside me, walking with me to the bedroom and thwarting my plans to take the test right away. Hurrying me along, he pulled the coat off me then tossed it onto the bed before taking my hand and pulling me with him. "Come on, let's go now."

My eyes held fast to the coat and the contents of the pocket. "I should hang that up, Galen."

"Nonsense, the maids will do that." He pulled me along, and I could do nothing but pray that no one would rummage through my pockets.

Down the stairs we went, then through room after room until we arrived at the playroom. I hadn't seen this room before. It was filled with toys of all kinds and video games as well as a pool table and even a pinball machine. And there was his brother and his brother's family.

"Brax, Pamala," Galen called out, making the couple turn to look up at us. "Here she is."

His brother appeared to be only a couple of years older than me. His wife looked even younger than me, and she carried a baby on her hip even as a two-year-old ran from one thing to another. The thing that stuck out the most about Galen's baby brother was the blonde hair that hung in loose waves to the middle of his back.

"Hey Ariel, it's nice to meet you. Galen just told us the news. Man, I had no idea my big bro was seeing anyone." And then I noticed that Brax lacked the Irish accent that Galen and his parents had.

I extended a hand to him. He took it, then pulled me in for a hug. "Oh, okay." I looked over his shoulder as his wife smiled.

She tapped him on the shoulder. "Okay, Brax, my turn." He stepped back and Pamala took over. "It's so good to meet you. I was beginning to wonder if Galen would ever bring a girl home."

Although young, she seemed to have known the family for a while. "Your children are adorable." I ran my hand over the baby boy's blonde curls. "And your name is?"

Pamala filled me in, "This is Ty, and that little monkey over there is Blake."

When the baby reached out for me, I drew in a breath. "You want me?"

Pamala handed him over to me, even though I wasn't ready in the least. "Here you go. He's a real charmer, just like the rest of the Dunne men, so watch out. He loves to give kisses."

Galen wrapped his arm around me then kissed my cheek. "Just like me."

"How old is he?" I asked.

"Six months," Brax said. "Nearly old enough to get on my surf-board with me."

Pamala shook her head. "No, he's not." She turned her attention to me. "Brax is a pro surfer. We live in Hawaii most of the time. When we're not there, we're in L.A. We've got a beach house in Malibu, just like Barbie and Ken." She laughed, so I did, too.

Brax and Galen walked away, so I took the opportunity to ask Pamala a few questions. "So how long have you and Brax been married?"

"Only a year." She showed me her amazing wedding set—diamonds upon diamonds. "But we've been together since the seventh grade. He and I were in the same private school together in L.A. He'd moved out there that year to start surfing lessons; he always wanted to be a surfer, if you can imagine that. He even got rid of his Irish accent and gained the surfer one you hear today."

"What a transformation. I can't imagine losing my accent." I looked at the brothers, who were so far apart in age. "What is Brax, twenty-three or so?"

"Twenty-two. And I'm nineteen." She smiled. "Yeah, I got knocked up by my love when I was sixteen. That was one rough year."

"I bet." I thought about how hard that must've been for her and him both. "How did your families take it? I imagine some could make things even more difficult for their kids if they found them in that situation."

"Mine did, his didn't. And Galen was our saving grace. He gave us the Malibu house and set us up with what he called 'the baby fund.' Without Galen, things would've really sucked." She patted me on the shoulder. "He's a nice guy. I know he's not the most romantic man, and he's never been great with commitment when it comes to women, but he's a nice person. He's never hurt anyone intentionally. You get what I'm saying?"

She thought he might drop me someday and just wanted to give me the head's up. "I'm aware of his past. And I'm aware of his tendency to find something else more interesting than the person he's with. But I'm hoping to keep him interested in me." I held up my crossed fingers, and she grinned at me.

"Good. I'm glad you're aware of his habits. I hate to see anyone come into Galen's life who's unaware of who he is in a relationship." Ty stirred in my arms and reached out to his mother, so I gave him back to her as a horde of people came into the room. "Oh, the sisters are here. Here we go."

By the sounds of chaos, I knew his sisters and their families would most likely be a bit overwhelming. "There're so many of them. How will I remember all of their names?"

"I say 'hon' a lot." Pamala led the way to start the massive introductions.

Galen came to my side, putting his arm around my shoulders. "Okay, this is Ariel Pendragon. She's from London. I hired her to work at Paradise Resort as my personal maid, so no jokes about servants. She's quite gifted in photography, so don't be surprised if you catch her taking pictures." He looked at me. "Anything else they should know about you, baby?"

With a shrug, I said, "I think you've covered all the bases."

And then more chaos ensued as names were called out, children pointed to, and then some adults, too. There were way too many people for me to hold onto any one name. At the end of the introductions, I announced, "If I call you a name that's not your own, please correct me."

They all laughed, which I found surprisingly welcoming. And then I had the sudden urge to relieve myself. As soon as Galen let me go so he could talk to his brothers-in-law, I made my escape.

Might as well use this opportunity to take the test—there's no better time than the present.

Hurrying up the stairs, I headed straight for the bedroom, only to find the maid cleaning it. "Oh, I'm sorry. I don't mean to get in your way." I noticed the coat had already been put away. "Is the coat you found on the bed in the closet?"

"Yes it is." She jerked her head toward the lavatory. "Stella is currently cleaning in there."

She must've noticed the pee dance I was doing. "Oh."

I looked at the closet and hurried to it to retrieve the brown paper bag. She'd put it in the far back corner, and it took me a minute to find it. Placing my hand in the pocket, I found the bag and pulled it out. Hiding it underneath my shirt, I left the closet.

There were three more lavatories in his wing, so I set off to find another one. Any one of them would do, I supposed.

Some romantic part of me wanted to take the test in the lavatory we'd showered in together and had made love in—what better place to get the news than somewhere we'd already built great memories? If it was news of a baby, that is. I had this list of things I knew I would recall forever, like the place I bought the test, the place I took the test, the place where I would tell Galen we were going to have a baby. Like snapshots in my mind, they would play out for the rest of my life.

But those snapshots would never happen if I didn't suck it up and take the test.

CHAPTER 18

Galen

With Ariel gone, I found myself surrounded by a gang of in-laws. Logan, Mark, and Paul had formed a semicircle around me, prodding me for information on my relationship with Ariel. I shoved my hands into my pockets, rocked back on my heels and stood my ground. "No, really. That hasn't changed—still a bachelor for life. I swear."

My brothers-in-law had been after me to join them in the bliss—or lack thereof—of holy matrimony and procreation. Mark boasted, "You know that you're not really a man until you've been barfed on by a two-year-old, right, Galen?"

Before the laughter stopped, Paul added, "Or until you've held the hand of your laboring wife and found she has the strength of ten men as she squeezes your hand. But you're thankful it's your hand she's massacring instead of your manhood, the part of you that did that to her in the first place."

The thought alone made my cock twinge—and not in a pleasant way. "And you wonder why I want to stay just the way I am?"

Logan put his hand on my shoulder and spoke a bit softer, "But you're missing out on the great part about being a married man, Galen. The sex is off the charts."

I found that hard to believe. The sex I had with Ariel now was off the charts. But Mark soon informed me of what off the charts meant to them. "By 'off the charts', he means sex isn't on the charts at all." Again they all laughed at their misfortune, and I found it amazing.

Brax came up behind me, closing the circle around me. "Are they giving you the business, big bro?"

"As usual, they are." I was used to the playful banter of my in-laws and even expected it. "I've just been informed that sex is a far off dream for married couples. But I'm quite perplexed by that statement as each of you have a plethora of little heathens who all bear remarkable similarities to their fathers. So sex has to be in there somewhere."

Brax answered that for me, "You see, when you're a father, you're so damn tired all the time from lack of sleep and constant chaos that you don't even know when you're actually having sex. Then a few months later, your old lady hands you another pregnancy test, and you're supposed to act happy and smile then tell her how grateful you are for her and your ever-expanding family."

I had to admit, that one got to me. "Whoa. Now I really don't want to join this club."

Brax put his arm around my shoulders. "But you've got to join us one day. Our club needs new members. And our kids need more cousins."

"Not me. You'll have to look elsewhere for those." I held my hands up as if pushing them all away. "I have no desire to smell like baby puke all day. I have no plans to walk around like a zombie for weeks after a baby is born. Yes, I've been witness to each and every one of you doing that with each new baby. I mean, how do you guys never get used to bringing home a newborn? How hard can it be that you never figure out how to make it easier?"

Paul just laughed as he shook his head. "Oh, man, you've got no idea. You see, one baby might have colic, and that's one problem that keeps you up nights. Then another baby might have trouble taking a crap, and that's what keeps you up nights."

Logan took over, "Or perhaps your wife had a particularly hard birth and her stitches itch, especially at night. She'll toss and turn until you get up and get her something to put on the stitches to make it stop." He looked over his shoulder to make sure no one was paying any attention to us, especially his wife. "And let me tell you something about having to tend to your wife's tender parts after childbirth."

I held up my hands in surrender. "God, no!"

Mark took me by the shoulder. "No, you've got to hear this. The first time I had to help my wife with something 'downstairs' was only a week after the birth of our first child. She was crying in the bathroom, and I went in to see what was wrong. I found her sitting on the toilet with a handheld mirror, looking at her crotch. And let me tell you, when I saw what that mirror reflected, I nearly passed the fuck out."

All the men nodded as I felt the color draining out of my face. "You know you're talking about my sister's crotch, right?"

Mark smiled. "Yeah. Sorry about that. But I'd never loved her more than in that moment. To see what she'd gone through to bring our baby into the world." He shook his head, as if he were still in disbelief after all these years.

Despite that one positive, I was still feeling overwhelmed by this onslaught of information. I took a step back, wanting to give myself a bit more space, but the guys just moved in closer and closer until my back was against the wall right next to the door. "With all these horror stories you guys always tell me, I can't imagine why I'm still single."

Brax frowned at me. "Single? Then what's with bringing Ariel around if you're still single?"

"She and I know where we stand." I wasn't about to get into the reality of my relationship with Ariel, especially not with these busybodies.

"And where is that?" Paul asked.

"Nowhere. We live in the moment. We do what we want to, and when we're done having fun, we'll move on." I put my hand into my pocket, playing with the black box I had in there. Ariel wouldn't be the only one surprised by my special Christmas Eve gift. My family, especially my brother and brothers-in-law, would be stupefied.

Brax looked a bit peeved. "Then why bring her around, dude?" Him and that silly surfer talk.

"What's it hurting?" I asked with a grin.

"The girls are going to get close to her. Your mother is going to get close to her. And what about the kids?" Logan was clearly just getting started on the topic, making me regret my teasing words. "What if they get close to her and love her, and the next time we see you, she's not with you, and then they ask about her, and you tell them you just got tired of her? No more Aunt Ariel, the beautiful redhead from London."

I laughed. "Glad to know you think she's beautiful."

Brax shook his head. "For real, dude. It's not cool to bring someone around family if you don't think she might become more than a bedroom buddy."

That he didn't realize that I actually did know better amazed me. I hadn't brought anyone home in over twenty years, what made them think I wasn't serious about Ariel?

But I kept it going anyway, knowing my midnight surprise would really knock everyone out of the park. "I don't think we have to worry about anyone here becoming too attached to her. We're leaving in a couple of days. Sure, Ma likes her fine, but she'll be okay when things end."

Paul's dark eyes grew in size. "Do you really believe that? 'Cause I can tell you otherwise. Once your mother came to visit for the weekend, and we were taking in a cat for the neighbors while they were on vacation. Your mother kept that cat with her the whole weekend, petting it, feeding it treats. I suppose no one told her that we were only cat-sitting. A few months later she came back to spend another weekend, and when she found the cat gone, she cried. I mean, actual tears, man. What's she going to do when she finds out the woman she thought might become her daughter-in-law is out of the picture?"

"I think you guys are getting ahead of the game." I wasn't sure how much longer I could let them go on. I'd started to feel bad about the little trick I was playing on them.

Brax shook his head. "You know how Ma was with Pamala. She took her under her wing when her family dumped on her for being pregnant so young. Ma is a real woman's woman. And she told me that she already adores Ariel." His eyes went big as he exclaimed, "Adores her, dude!"

It felt good to know that my mother shared my feelings about Ariel. She hadn't told me anything that specific. At least now I knew our matriarch would welcome my surprise. I played with the box in my pocket again.

Later that night I intended to sit on the fireplace and pull Ariel to sit on my lap, I was going to ask her for something I knew she would never see coming. And hopefully she would want the same thing I did, and we would have our happily ever after. And my family would all be overjoyed for us.

I could already picture how it would all unfold.

"You should try to keep her away from family things from now on, if you're not going to keep her around, Galen," Brax said with a frown.

Logan agreed, "Yeah, it's going to kill your mother."

"Ah, Ma will be fine. She's a tough old bird." I chuckled, knowing that later they would all know I was only kidding around with them. "Ariel knows what's up. I've been honest with her. She knows how I roll. When I find something else to take my attention, I move on. No reason to cry. No reason to be upset. That's just me. She gets it."

"Man, what a shame. You guys would make some gorgeous kids," Mark interjected. "You both have curls, and her hair is remarkable. Is it real or fake?"

"It's real, that's her natural auburn color." I thought we'd make gorgeous children, too. "But kids? No way. I don't see them in my future at all. Little barf machines: poopers, criers, beggars, and thieves. They steal your energy, time, and even your girl. No, kids aren't my thing, and neither is a wife. It's all about living life free as a bird. Too bad you guys don't get it."

"Mark, wipe Stanley's nose, will you?" my mother called out. "It's really nasty, and I can't get up. Samuel is insistent on staying on my lap."

"Where's Mindy?" Mark asked as he left our group.

All I could do was laugh. "Oh, yeah, tell me again how great it is to be a husband and father."

Brax and the others sighed, and our little group broke up as the men all went to tend to their broods. All the while, I leaned back against the wall, thinking how surprised everyone was going to be when the clock struck midnight.

This Christmas will be one for the books.

CHAPTER 19

Ariel

The first lavatory door I opened smelled too much of cleaning agent, so I closed that door, not wanting that smell to get lodged in my memory. I headed to the back of the hallway and opened the next door down the way. And there I found a perfect place to do the test.

There was a window was at the end of the room and I could see snowflakes wafting past. A large evergreen tree blew in the breeze, and it looked like Christmas out that window. All that was missing was Santa and his sleigh pulled by eight tiny reindeer.

I could look out that window from my seat on the toilet, too. Now, this was the kind of memory I was talking about. This would be an excellent thing to think back on.

I could just imagine sitting in a rocking chair, holding our first child on my lap and telling him the story of the first day we learned about him. I would tell him that it was Christmas Eve and about how I'd had to sneak out to pick up the test from Ben's Pharmaceuticals. Then I would tell him how beautiful the falling snow looked and how the wind blew a tree back and forth.

It was already becoming a wonderful image in my mind. As I finally peed on the stick, I found myself actually hoping for a positive result.

I would have to wait five minutes, but even that small amount of time seemed like an eternity.

Pacing back and forth, I finally went to the window and placed my forehead against the cold glass. "I might be a mother, Mum. I hope I can be as good a one as you were. I'll try to be even better, if you don't mind. I love you. I miss you. And Dad, too. It'll be good to have a family again. I just hope Galen will be as pleased as I am about this." I paused. "Listen to me, talking as if I already know I'm having a baby."

I looked over my shoulder at the stick that sat on the edge of the sink. If I wasn't pregnant, then would I venture so far as to ask Galen if we could have a baby?

My hands folded over my stomach. It hadn't ever been completely flat, except when I was living on the streets in London. Before that, it had always been a bit round. After going to work at the resort and eating everything I wanted when I wanted, it had gone back to that little round state. Nothing huge, just a little bump.

I imagined that bump growing larger as a baby grew inside of me. The thought made me happier than I ever thought it could. I wish I could've known for certain if Galen would feel the same way.

If he and I had ever had a real talk about having a family, I would've felt a lot better about this. But the fact that we hadn't— other than our brief comments the night before—weighed on me. I had no idea if the man ever wanted children. And I hadn't been around him and his nephews and nieces long enough to see how he interacted with children and babies.

In my mind, Galen would make an exceptional father. He had patience and understanding, two things I knew a good parent must have. He'd already proven himself as a more than a great provider for a family. And the way he'd treated me when I'd first arrived at the island proved to me that he was the kind of man who would stand by his woman during tough times. I could imagine suffering through labor with him at my side. We'd hold hands, and he would say just the right things to comfort me as I went through that difficult process.

My daydream shattered as the timer on my cell went off. The five minutes was up, and the time had come to see if I'd be having Galen Dunne's baby.

My feet felt heavy as I walked back to the sink. My eyes closed on their own, as if not wanting to know the results just yet. I whispered, "Lord, let this be whatever you want for me. I will accept this no matter the result." My hands fisted. "But I'd really like to have a baby."

I opened my eyes and looked down to find a plus sign. Tears immediately clouded my vision, making me wonder if I'd seen it right. I grabbed some tissue off the counter to wipe the tears out of my eyes, then picked up the stick and looked at it again.

"It's positive! I'm having a baby!" My hand shook, then the rest of my body joined in, and I had to take a seat on the edge of the bathtub. "We're having a baby. Galen and I are having a baby. Oh, God. I've got to tell him."

I nearly shoved the stick into the pocket of my sweater then shuddered as I recalled what was on the thing. Wrapping it in a few tissues, I then placed it in the pocket before washing my hands.

Slowly, I walked out of the lavatory, ready to tell Galen everything. Taking deep breaths, I had to try to keep myself in check. I didn't want to rush into the room full of Dunnes and announce that Galen and I were having a baby. I had to tell the father first, after all.

Just as I came to the door to the playroom I heard Galen's deep voice, "With all these horror stories you guys always tell me, I can't imagine why I'm still single." I stopped in my tracks to listen.

I heard another man's voice asking the question I wanted to know, too. "Single? Then what's with bringing Ariel around if you're still single?"

I leaned up against the wall just outside the door, my heart starting to hurt.

Galen replied, "She and I know where we stand."

I thought I'd known approximately where we stood, but had I

been way off base?

"And where is that?" another guy asked. I went stiff as I waited for Galen's response.

"Nowhere. We live in the moment. We do what we want to, and when we're done having fun, we'll move on," Galen's words had deflated me entirely.

I stayed plastered to the wall, unable to move as each new assertion Galen made tore at my heart a little more. It was like looking at a car crash—I couldn't tear myself away. It was as if everything stood still and yet sped up, as I felt my whole world crashing around me.

As I stood there listening to Galen tear apart our relationship, telling his family that I meant nothing to him, I felt a strange sense of detachment. I must've started zoning out, but then reality crashed back to me as I heard someone mention babies.

"Kids? No way. I don't see them in my future at all. Little barf machines: poopers, criers, beggars, and thieves. They steal your energy, time, and even your girl. No, kids aren't my thing, and neither is a wife. It's all about living life free as a bird. Too bad you guys don't get it."

Free as a bird?

"Mark, wipe Stanley's nose, will you?" I heard Felicity call out. "It's really nasty, and I can't get up. Samuel is insistent on staying on my lap."

"Where's Mindy?" the guy I now knew was Galen's brother-in-law Mark asked about his wife's whereabouts.

Galen just laughed. "Oh, yeah, tell me again how great it is to be a husband and father."

Well, I guess you'll never get the chance to find out, Galen Dunne!

As quietly as I could, I turned away and then ran swiftly back to his wing and up to his bedroom. I was thankful that the maids had finished cleaning so I could pack my bags.

There was no reason to waste any more time with the man. He obviously hadn't changed a bit since the start of our relationship—if I could even call it that now—and some part of me knew I'd only been fooling myself. But he'd fooled me, too.

I thought he might actually be starting to love me. And I knew I loved him. We hadn't said it yet, but it was right there. I'd already resolved to tell him that I loved him when I told him the news about the baby.

Now, he would never know about my love or our baby. I'd already heard with my own ears what his reaction would be to learning he'd made a child. It was clear the man wanted no part of this baby's life—or mine.

Taking my cell out of my pocket, I called a taxi and told them to meet me at Ben's Pharmaceuticals. I wasn't going to have a car pull up to the house and have a whole morbid scene play out in front of Galen's family. I cared too much for them to do that.

Carrying my bag and my purse, I walked out of the room with no intention of telling Galen a thing. But then I thought about his family, and I didn't want them to worry about me.

Going back into his bedroom, I found a pen and paper in the top dresser drawer and wrote a short note.

Galen,

I'm leaving. Tell your mother I said thank you for the hospitality. This is not anyone's fault but your own. If you replay the events and conversations you've had today, I'm sure you will realize why I left. Also, I quit. I think we'd both be better off if you just forget that you ever knew me. It shouldn't be hard for a man like you.

I didn't sign it. I left it on the table next to his side of the bed. The bed we'd made love in every night we'd been there.

After a freezing walk to the pharmacy, I found the cab waiting for me. Before I got in, I went to the trash bin outside the store and tossed my cell phone into it. I didn't want there to be any way for Galen to contact me, to try to talk me into going back to the resort—or worse, to try to make me believe he felt any way other than what I'd heard him express with my own ears.

Or maybe he'd fess up and say he was done with me. Whatever it would be, I didn't want to hear it. I didn't want to hear his voice ever again. I couldn't take it if I did.

No. From that moment on, it would just be me and my baby.

CHAPTER 20

Galen

I had no idea where Ariel had gotten off to, and after a little while of not seeing her, I knew I had to go looking for her. It was a big house, and she might've been lost in the place.

Pulling out my cell, I called her, knowing she kept hers on her all the time. It went straight to voicemail, so I thought she might be up in our room taking a nap or something and had turned it off.

Heading up the stairs, I hoped she wasn't coming down with a cold or something. She'd been eating lightly and didn't want any alcohol, so I thought she might not be feeling well. And I hated the fact that she didn't feel comfortable enough with me to tell me anything about it.

Opening the door to our bedroom, I found it empty. "Ariel?"

I went to the bathroom to see if she was in there, but that room was empty too. "Ariel?"

It occurred to me that she might've decided to go back outside for a walk or something, so I went to check the closet for the coat she'd bought when we first got to Portland. My heart went to my throat when I opened that door. "No."

The closet was empty. She'd had dresses, shoes, winter clothes, a coat, and sweaters. Nothing was there. Not even her purse. "What the hell?"

Spinning around, I looked all over the room for any sign of where she might've taken all of her things. I hoped she'd just moved them to another room for some odd reason, and I raced around to look in each room in my wing to see if she or her things were in any of them. But there was nothing.

My head spun out of control as I went back to our room and looked carefully over everything once more. She had to have left something behind that would give me a hint of what the hell she was doing.

And then I noticed something just underneath the bed. It must have fallen to the floor, and the edge of it barely peeked out from under the bedspread. I leaned down to pick it up and found it was a notepad with handwriting on it.

I quickly scanned her words, then fell on the bed as all the air left my lungs, reading it a second time more slowly. "She's gone?"

How could she leave without talking to me?

She must have heard me joking with the guys. I hadn't meant a word I'd said. It was all a ploy to throw everyone off. But it had all been pointless, because I wouldn't be surprising anyone now that Ariel was no longer there.

She had to be going to the airport, that much I knew. I ran to the closet to get my coat, putting it on as I ran down the stairs. I saw Brax in the kitchen as I passed through. "Tell everyone I'll be back soon. I've got to run out and get something."

"Hey, hold up, dude. I'll come with," he called out after me.

I had no intentions of letting my family know that Ariel had left. "No. I'll be back soon."

Heading to the garage, I grabbed the first set of car keys on the board. Hopping into the BMW, I set out to get my woman back.

Even though it was Christmas Eve and no one should have to work, the snowplows were keeping the falling snow from accumulating on the roads. But that didn't make it any easier to get to the airport as fast as I wanted to.

I knew Ariel had plenty of money to get wherever she wanted. But I didn't know where she wanted to go. She'd quit as my maid, so I doubted she would go back to the resort.

Will she go to London?

Where else did she know? Would she go back to the streets?

Surely not. She had money, and she had a great reference if she wanted to be a maid somewhere else. Why go back to the streets if you have all that?

The airport came into view, and I stepped on the gas. I needed to get inside and find her.

She's got to be here.

Dropping the Beemer in valet parking, I went inside. I stopped the first airport person I saw. "Is there a flight leaving for London, England today?" I asked.

The lady pointed up at the Departures board. "It left fifteen minutes ago. Seems you missed it. It had been delayed, but the snow let up just long enough for it to take off."

All I could do was stand there, staring at that damn board. "She's gone."

My head swiveled around until I saw no line at one of the ticket agent's booths. I slowly made my way to the agent. I was fairly sure there was no way she'd tell me a thing about anyone, and I knew that, but I had to try. "Ma'am, can you help me, please?"

She looked up from her computer keyboard. "Yes, sir. What can I help you with today?"

"The flight to London that just left, can you tell me if a woman named Ariel Pendragon was on it?" I crossed my fingers, but the look on the woman's face told me that wasn't going to work.

She shook her head. "I'm sorry, sir. It's against our privacy policy to divulge any of our customer's information."

"It's very important," I begged.

"I'm sure it is." She could only smile at me. "But I can't help you. My advice is to head home and try to enjoy your Christmas."

Turning to leave, I knew I couldn't enjoy anything until I found her and told her everything. "Please. I was going to ask her to marry me at midnight. She overheard the wrong conversation and now she thinks I don't want a wife. She ran away, and I can't take any of it back. I can't tell her how I really feel."

The woman's expression must've changed because it prompted her coworker to speak up, "That doesn't matter, Zelda. You still can't tell him anything."

I considered making one more plea, but they both turned away to an airport console. There was no hope left. Now all I could do was go back home, pray she answers her phone, and make plans to go to London in the morning on my jet. I would scour that city until I found her.

As I walked out to the valet, I tried texting her: You've got to call me. What you overheard was a joke. I swear to God, it was all a joke. Call me, and I will explain everything to you. I love you, Ariel Pendragon. Please call me.

I thought about adding in that I wanted to marry her, but decided against it. If she read the text, she'd call me. I knew she would. She would give me the chance to explain things to her.

The girl loved me, I knew it. And she knew it, even though we'd never said it. I would give her the world if she'd let me, which I knew she wouldn't. She would want to get that all on her own. And I loved that about her.

As I drove back home, I wondered how I was going to explain Ariel's absence to everyone without making her seem like a flighty person who had little to no faith in me.

I couldn't even come up with a lie about her getting an urgent phone call from her family in London and taking off. I'd already told my family her whole backstory. They all knew she'd been living in the streets when her mother passed away. And they knew her father was dead, too. So what was I going to tell them about why she'd left?

As I walked into the kitchen after parking the car, I found my mother speaking to the cook about what she wanted for the Christmas Eve festivities. "Those tiny rolled up tortilla things with cream cheese and radishes. You know what I'm talking about. I want a platter of those and something for the kids. But no sugar. None at all. They're already quite the handful." Ma's eyes cut to me. "Galen, where've you been? And where's Ariel? I want to show her pictures of you when you were a boy."

How I wished she could've done that. "Ma, she's gone." I gulped as my legs went weak, and I had to hurry to sit on a bar stool before I fell down.

"Gone?" Ma came to my side. "Galen, why are you so pale? Where's she gone to?"

"I'm not sure. London, I suspect." I looked into my mother's pale green eyes, and they reminded me of Ariel's. "Ma, I was joking with the lads, and she must've overheard me. I had no idea, or I would've told her the truth." I pulled the black box out of my pocket and handed it to her. "I was kidding around with the boys about not being the marrying kind and stuff like that. But I was going to ask her to marry me at midnight tonight. But now I can't." I pulled the note Ariel had left me and handed it to my mother. "This is all she left."

She read it, then looked at me with sadness in her eyes. "Oh, son, what have ya done?"

"Ma, I know." I couldn't hold it back any longer. I grabbed my mother and hugged her tight as I cried. "I've got to find her. She has my heart. I can't live without that."

"No, ya can't." She patted me on the back. "She loves you, I know it. She'll call when her anger has settled. You'll see. She'll call ya."

I pray she does.

CHAPTER 21

Ariel

The Jumeirah Carlton Tower Hotel in London became my hideaway. Thanks to the hefty wages I'd made while working at the resort, my bank account was heavily padded. Since Galen had helped me set up my bank account when I first went to work at his resort, I'd been smart enough to get the account number changed so he couldn't track my expenses and find me.

The day after Christmas had been a busy one for me. I'd called the bank first thing that morning, then cracked open my laptop to search for a job. I had plenty of money to see me through for months, but only if I could find a flat with reasonable rent. I needed to save that money for when the baby came. Staying in the five-star hotel was only a temporarily solution if I wanted that money to last me a while.

I could've gone to a cheap place, but I figured why should I punish myself? I hadn't done a thing wrong, Galen had. The more I thought about it, the more I wondered just how much longer the man had been planning to keep me around. By the things he'd said, not too much longer was my guess.

As I looked over the employment ads online, I found that there were openings for housekeepers right in the hotel I was staying at. A job at a place this fancy would undoubtedly come with a nice salary and maybe some perks, too.

But I can't let Nova know where the inquiry is coming from if she's to be my reference.

How could I possibly obtain a job at such a fine establishment if I couldn't allow them to contact my former employer?

But I did have my banking information, and it showed the weekly deposits from Paradise Resort if I needed to prove past employment. Hopefully, that would be enough to get me in the door with the hotel. Gaining employment was my top priority. I had more than just myself to think about now. My baby had to have a place to live. And I needed to be able to care for myself during my pregnancy to make sure I had a healthy baby.

Dressing in a black skirt and white shirt, I put on a pair of flats, put my hair in a bun at the nape of my neck, then went down to the lobby to ask for the manager. "Excuse me." I said to the woman at the front desk.

"Oh, I'm sorry," she apologized. "What can I do for you?"

"I'd like to speak with the manager about the housekeeping job that was posted. Do you know when I could get an appointment with him or her?" I asked.

She shook her head. "He's not due back from holiday until next Monday. But I can certainly put you down on his list of appointments." She typed on her computer. "He's open at ten-thirty on Monday morning. Can you make that?"

"I can." I pulled my wallet out. "Can I pay for the next week in advance? I'm in room two-fifteen, under Ariel Pendragon."

She looked surprised. "You're staying here at our hotel?"

"I am." I pulled out my bank card. "Is that a problem?"

"No," she shook her head as she took my card to make the transaction. "It's just that our rates aren't cheap, and someone who's looking for a job in housekeeping usually can't afford to stay here."

"I had a lucrative job at an island resort before. It's put plenty of padding in my bank account." I hoped by letting the woman know of my experience it would gain me some footing when the manager came back. Perhaps she'd put in a good word for me.

Pushing the receipt to me to sign, she asked, "Why did you leave this resort, if I might ask?"

I didn't know exactly what to say, but came up with something quickly. "Life on a tiny island just got to me is all. I'm from London originally, and I wanted to get back home."

"I can see that." She looked me over then asked, "Since you're staying here, I assume you have no one in London to stay with."

"No, I have no one to stay with here." I found myself looking down, feeling the urge to cry. I was alone again without Galen. The loneliness wasn't a welcome feeling. "I'll be looking for a flat to rent once I gain employment and know how much I'll be bringing in."

She handed me my receipt. "You know, if you get this job, you're eligible to stay here, on the top floor. One of our perks is housing in the suites up there. It's a small living room and kitchen with one bedroom and a lavatory. There's a charge, but it's much less than the rent of any flat in town."

"That sounds like a dream come true. Living and working right here would be similar to how things were on the island." Of course, I'd had a whole bungalow there, but this would be great, too.

She nodded. "I lived here for three years when I first started working at the hotel. When I got married, I moved out. Another perk is the free meals. We get one free meal during our shift. And breakfast is always free, as we have that for our guests and staff are welcome to the buffet, too. All in all, we've got a pretty great deal here."

"It sounds almost as good as what I've left behind." And just saying that I'd left something behind made my heart ache. I didn't want to think that I'd left Galen behind me. He would've left me eventually anyway.

"You know what? I think I can put in a call to Mr. Bagwell, the manager. I'm the assistant manager, and I might be able to hire you on before he gets back." She eyed me as she smiled. "Can you tell me where you worked before?"

Chewing my lip, I finally said, "Paradise Resort in the Caribbean. Have you heard of it?"

She shook her head. "No. What company owns it?"

"It's not a company. It's more of a private resort owned by one man. And he invites the guests. It's very exclusive, and typically caters to the ultrawealthy. And I wouldn't be able to let anyone make an inquiry about me to the manager." I knew that didn't sound good and flinched a bit.

Her expression told me she thought that odd. "Were you let go, or did you leave on your own?"

"I left on my own. I had my reasons." I didn't want this to get in my way of getting the job, but figured I had to say something about it. "Look, I left for very personal reasons. I can show you the deposits on my bank account to prove that I did work there. Would that help?"

"It might." She wrote something on a piece of paper then pushed it toward me. "I'm Cherry. I'll see if Mr. Bagwell can be reached, and then I'll let you know what he says. This is the pay rate for the job. Is this something you could live with?"

I looked at the small yellow paper with a number three times less than what I was making at the island. But with the lower rent and free meals, I could get by. "Yes, that rate is fine with me. As long as I can get the low rent living quarters here."

"There're a few vacancies. I'm sure you can get in. And if you're hired, you'll be refunded for the price of the room you're in now, and we can get you moved into your new place as soon as you sign the employment paperwork." Someone came up behind me, so our chat had to end. "I'll give you a call on your room phone when I find something out, Miss Pendragon."

"Thank you. And please call me Ariel." As I turned to leave, I felt a bit better than I had before I'd come down to see about the job. At least I had something to look forward to now.

Stopping at the breakfast buffet, I knew I had to eat, even though I had no appetite to speak of. I hadn't slept well without Galen holding me. I missed that damn man so badly it was taking a physical toll.

He didn't want me anymore. Why can't I just put him out of my mind?

Placing some fresh fruit on my plate, I decided I'd stick to a healthy diet to keep myself in the best health possible. I knew that stress could affect my immune system in a bad way, so I vowed to my baby that I would try my best to stay healthy, despite how I felt.

Sitting at a table with a glass of apple juice, I noticed a woman looking at me, and then she waved at me. "Excuse me, I'm sorry for staring. It's just that your hair color and those green eyes are quite memorable. I've seen you before."

My life on the streets seemed to be coming back to haunt me. "Have you?" I recognized the lady then and felt a rush of panic for some reason.

"You and another woman were in my shop a little less than a year ago. She collapsed. I recall it as if it was yesterday." She got up and came to sit with me at the small table. "I've thought about you two often. You seem fine now, but how is she?"

"I remember you. You were very nice to us." I reached out to touch the top of her hand, which she'd placed on the table. "Thank you for calling for help for her. We had no idea at the time that my mother had advanced cancer. She passed several months ago. Thanks to you, she did so under the care of physicians, instead of dying on the streets."

She looked away as her eyes clouded with tears. "I'm so sorry. You don't know how much you two have been on my mind." She looked at me as she wiped her eyes with a napkin. "And how have you gotten on?"

"My mother's doctor called a friend of his, who gave me an outstanding job on a resort." I thought about how Galen had stuck his neck out for me, and it made me feel guilty about leaving him without giving him a chance to say goodbye.

"Sounds like you found good luck after all that time on the streets." She frowned as she looked at the table. "I'd seen you two on the streets before you came in. I knew you had nowhere to go. I could've offered you both jobs at my shop. Instead, I chose to ignore you. I'm so sorry. What's your name?" She looked back up at me.

"Ariel," I told her. "And I don't want you to feel guilty about anything. Things happen for reasons we're not supposed to understand." Like having a baby alone because the man you love is incapable of loving anyone.

"I'm Abigail. And like I said, I own that shop." She put her purse on the table then unzipped it and took out a small business card and a pen. She wrote something on the card then handed it to me. "If you're in the market for a job, I can give you one. Plus, I've added some free credit for any merchandise you'd like to purchase in my shop."

Looking at the amount of free credit she'd given me, I shook my head. "I can't accept this. It's very generous, and I do appreciate the thought. But I managed to make good money while employed at the resort. I'm no longer in need of any extra help, but the job would be appreciated. I'm looking to get a job in housekeeping here at this hotel, but a second job would be welcomed. Can I call you after I find out if I have this job and what shift I'll be on? We can work something out after I know that."

"Yes, of course." She smiled at me, so widely I couldn't believe it. It was as if I'd made her day or something, and I didn't see how that could be. She was the one offering me a favor. "Ariel, I've been kicking myself since your mother fell at my shop for not doing something for you two. Letting me give you a job will help me get past that guilt."

"Truly, I do wish you wouldn't feel guilt over anything." It was clear that she was a very empathetic person, and she seemed like she would be a great employer.

"I have to feel guilt, Ariel." She ran the back of her hand over her cheeks as tears trickled down them. "I saw people who needed help and did nothing."

Between her and the loss of Galen, my heart ached so badly that I knew it wasn't good for the baby I carried. "I never blamed you or anyone else for our problems. But if it helps you at all, I forgive you, Abigail."

I didn't want to carry sadness or resentment in my heart, but I knew forgiving Galen would be much harder.

I wonder if I can ever forgive Galen for what he's done.

22

CHAPTER 22

Galen

The moist London air had me pulling my coat tighter around me as I got off my jet. This was the fifth trip to the town I'd made, and despite my lack of results, I felt sure that this was where Ariel was hiding. Two months had passed since she'd left me. One might think I'd begun to grow weary of hunting her down, but one would be wrong.

I'd made a commitment to find the woman, no matter how long it took. I wasn't going to move on and forget about her. That wasn't even possible.

My dreams were filled with her. And as much as the memory of her made my heart ache, it gave me the fuel to keep seeking her out. To see her pretty face and beautiful smile again—in reality, instead of a dream—was my only goal.

London wasn't the only place I had searched. I searched Portland to make sure she hadn't just gone to some hotel there to get away from me. I went to the island to see if she'd stopped by there to pick up the rest of her things and found she had not.

Ariel didn't know much about any other places other than those three. So I'd narrowed it down to London—she had to be there. And I wasn't leaving town until I found her this time around.

Heading to the office of the private investigator I'd hired just before arriving, I found Dwayne Layton sitting at a desk drinking coffee. His little office reeked of it. "You Dunne?" He didn't bother getting up.

"I am." I walked over to the coffee pot to pour myself a cup. "Mind?"

"No, go ahead." He picked up a pen and put it to a yellow pad of paper. "You said it's been a couple of months since you've seen her, right?"

"Yeah," I filled a small cup with the black liquid, then took a seat in front of his desk. "Two months. Her name is Ariel Gail Pendragon. She's twenty-two. Her birthday was on January seventeenth. Her natural hair color is auburn, her eyes emerald green. She's got fair, creamy skin and is five feet three inches. Her frame is small, and she's curvaceous."

He stopped writing to look me in the eyes. "I know this sounds crass, but big tits?"

I nodded. "Double D's. And an ass that won't quit. She's a head-turner. But I have a feeling she may have dyed her hair and might even be wearing contacts to hide the color of her eyes. She apparently really wants to stay hidden from me. I had her cell phone tracked down and found it in a dumpster in Portland. That's where she left me: Portland, Oregon. She'd tossed it into the trash bin in front of a pharmacy."

"And you said that she ran off because she overheard you saying some insensitive things that were taken out of context." He eyed me carefully. "And nothing more than that?"

"Nothing more than that." I took a sip of the hot coffee and grimaced at the strong acrid taste.

"You never hurt her in any way?" He wouldn't stop eyeing me.

"I have never hurt her. Only by my words that day, and that wasn't intentional." I looked over my shoulder to see if I'd missed any sugar that might've been by the coffee machine, but found none. "Look, what I need from you is help. I'll do my part and then some. She most likely has a job in housekeeping somewhere. But that could be anywhere from hospitals to hotels."

"How about waitressing?" he asked as he jotted down what I'd said.

"I doubt she'd do that kind of work. She's the kind of person who sticks with what she knows." I thought about the camera I'd given her and knew she'd taken it with her. "We might look at photo studios to see if they have any stills that she might've put on commission."

His expression turned puzzled. "A housekeeper who takes professional photographs?"

"Well, she was getting very good at photography and was working toward it as a career. I don't want to leave any stone unturned, just in case." I took another sip of the nasty coffee to help ease the jetlag. "I've got to find her, Mr. Layton. I'm not leaving until I do. I've got a suite at the Millennium in Knightsbridge."

He cocked his head as he wrote that down. "You should check out that whole area down there. I'll check out the Piccadilly Circus area since you've said she used to live on the streets around there."

"That sounds good to me." I got up, taking my coffee and pouring it out in the small sink next to the coffee machine. "The sooner you can get on that, the better."

"I happen to have nothing but time at present. I'll get on it this afternoon." He rubbed his temples. "This isn't a small town. I want you to know that it may take a while to find her. If she's changed her name and her appearance, it may take a very long time. Are you prepared for that?"

Not really.

I stuffed my hands into my pockets. "Look, I can't stop until I find her. If it takes forever, I'll never stop looking."

He nodded, then I left him to get to his part of the job. I wanted to get checked in at the hotel, get a nap, then a shower to wake myself up thoroughly before starting my search. I wanted to have my wits about me when I went looking for her.

Even upon checking into my hotel, I asked the lady at the front desk, "Does Ariel Pendragon work here by any chance?"

"Who?" the woman asked, typing like crazy on her computer.

"Ariel Pendragon. Curly auburn hair, emerald green eyes." I pulled the credit card out of my wallet as she took a moment to think about it.

Finally, she shook her head. "No. We don't have anyone matching that description here. We do have a redhead, but she's around fifty. That's not her, I would guess."

"No. Ariel's twenty-two. You might've seen her around town. Five-three, curvy?" I tried to get the woman to really search her memory.

But nothing came from it. "No. I don't recall anyone who looks like that. But then again, I'm not one to remember everyone I pass by on the streets."

And there were so many people on the streets that it made it hard to pick anyone out. I knew I had my work cut out for me. "You did set me up in a luxury suite, right?"

"Yes, sir." She swiped my card then handed me the keycard to my room. "Top floor, sir. Enjoy your stay with us."

She had no idea how unenjoyable my stay would be until I found the woman I loved. "Thanks. Let's hope it's not a long one." I prayed I would find her soon. I needed to see Ariel, to hear her sweet voice, to hold her.

Once I got up to my room, I fell on the bed in a heap. The ride over from Portland must've really taken a toll on me because I didn't wake up until the next morning. The maid tapping on my door woke me up. "Maid service," came a British accent.

In my sleep-hazed mind, she sounded like Ariel, and it had me springing out of bed and rushing to the door. But when I opened it, I found a short blonde standing there, looking at me like she thought I might be crazy. "I don't need any maid service today. Thanks anyway."

She ducked her head as she pushed her cart toward the next room. "Very good, sir. You have a pleasant day."

I took the chance to ask her about Ariel. "Hey, you don't happen to know anyone named Ariel Pendragon, do you? She's got long, curly auburn hair and dark green eyes. They're so dark in color they look like emeralds."

"I've got a cousin who has those features, but her name isn't Ariel Pendragon." She smiled at me. "Are you looking for this woman for any certain reason?"

I thought she might actually know Ariel and might be trying to figure me out. "She's my girlfriend. She overheard me say some foolish things that I didn't mean and left without staying to talk about them. If I could just talk to her, I would get her to understand that I was just joking around. I love her."

She smiled as she ducked her head shyly. "How sweet. I don't know the woman, but if I ever meet anyone by that name, I will ask her if she's lost a handsome boyfriend."

"Please do." I grabbed a business card out of my pocket. "And here's my name and number if you do happen to find her. Please let me know if you do. I've got to find her. I'm not leaving London until I do."

She took the card, putting it away in her apron. "I promise you that I will call if I ever find this woman."

I decided to ask a little more from her. "If you ever see a woman in her early twenties who fits that description, please let me know as soon as possible so I can get to where she is and see if it's her. I am truly desperate."

"I can see that." She nodded at my wrinkled clothing. "If you'll put your clothes in the laundry bag and set it outside your door, we will pick it up and have the clothes cleaned and pressed for you. They'll be returned to your closet the next morning."

"Thanks." I smiled at her to make her feel comfortable with me. "I look forward to hearing from you. And your name is?"

"Oh, you would need that, wouldn't you?" She laughed a little. "I'm Clara."

"Okay, Clara, thank you so much for your help." I stepped back inside my room and closed the door. I needed a shower and a shave, then I needed to grab a bite before heading off to the other hotels in the area.

It took me no time at all to get ready, and I managed to grab a bagel and a bottle of juice from the hotel's morning buffet before leaving. Walking down the sidewalk, I made my way to the nearest hotel and found myself standing in front of the Jumeirah Carlton Tower Hotel. Finishing the last bite of the bagel then chugging the rest of the juice, I placed the empty bottle in the bin outside the door before going in.

It being morning, I knew the maids were busy cleaning the rooms for the day. This would be my best chance to see if Ariel was employed here. The thing about checking out the hotels in the area was that even if she didn't work there, she might've stayed at one of these when she first arrived. Someone might recognize her description if not her name.

Striding up to the front desk, I greeted the woman standing there. Her nametag told me her name was Cherry. "Good morning, Cherry. How are you doing this fine morning?"

Her smile was wide as she greeted me, "I'm lovely this morning. I hope you are, too. What can I help you with, sir?"

"I happen to be looking for a woman, Cherry. Her name is Ariel Pendragon. Would she happen to work at this fine establishment?" I gave her as broad a smile as she'd given me, trying to make her feel at ease.

Only she didn't look at ease at all. "Oh, sir, I can't."

The door behind her opened, and a gentleman walked out. "Hello, sir. Did I hear you asking after someone?"

"Yes." I had hoped he'd heard the name and was about to give me welcome news.

"We can't give out any information about our employees." He gave a nod to Cherry, and she went through the door he'd come out of and closed it behind her.

"So, she is an employee here," I said as I put my hands into my pockets to appear non-threatening.

"I didn't say that," he clarified. "I said that we couldn't tell you about anyone who works here. We can't answer any questions you might have, sir."

"It's simple yes or no, sir." I rocked on my heels to appear as if nothing was wrong, even though my entire body was on the verge of shaking. "You see, she and I were seeing each other. She misunderstood something she heard me saying."

He held up one hand. "Please, don't waste your breath. I will not answer you. We don't give out any information. None."

"I hear ya, man," I replied. "Thanks anyways." I turned around with the biggest smile I'd had since finding Ariel's note. He might not be able to give me a firm answer, but I knew in my gut that I was getting closer.

23

CHAPTER 23

Ariel

The smell of alcohol filled my nose as the nurse dabbed some on a cotton ball then ran it over the inside of my wrist. "We'll get a little blood sample from you to get things going, Miss Pendragon. Will the baby's father be joining you on the next visit? You'll be in the beginning of your second trimester then and can have a sonogram done. That's usually when we can tell you what gender you'll be having."

My first prenatal visit was going well, better than I'd expected. But I hadn't counted on anyone asking me about the baby's father. "At this time, and most likely for the duration, the baby's father won't be involved."

The nurse was all of fifty, and her eyes took on a sad, compassionate expression. "I'm sorry to hear that."

The last two months had been lonelier than I had anticipated, and I found myself needing to confide in someone. "He doesn't want any children. Nor does he want a wife or even a girlfriend." I sniffled a little, telling myself that I wasn't going to cry about this at my first appointment. "I made a mistake. I trusted a man who had told me from the start that he didn't believe in love or relationships. So I'll be taking on the responsibility of being both parents to my child. He most likely wouldn't give me the time of day even if I did tell him about the baby."

The nurse picked up a long syringe then I turned my head so I wouldn't see her stick it into the vein on my wrist. "So you haven't told him about the baby? That's a tough situation, my dear. If you want my advice, I'd suggest at least letting him know, so long as he won't harm you or your child in any way. Most of the time it's better to tell the man, rather than have him find out after the baby's born. I've seen a few mothers in my time who were taken to court over not telling the fathers about their babies."

That would only be an issue if Galen ever went to the trouble of tracking me down, and I wasn't worried about that happening. "Thank you for your advice."

By the look on her face, I knew she realized it was a lost cause, but I didn't sense any judgment from her. "So, we'll take this blood, run some tests, then we'll give you the results when you come in next month. That'll be all for today."

"And the due date will be given to me then, I suppose," I said as I got up.

"It will." She opened the door of the examination room and walked out. "Follow me and I'll show you the way out through this maze of ours."

"Thank you." I followed her until I found myself in the waiting room once again.

The nurse put her hand on my shoulder before I could walk away. "Please think about what I've said to you, my dear."

I nodded but made no verbal promises. I'd gone nearly three months without telling Galen anything. The reality of raising this baby alone was getting easier and easier all the time.

Working much harder than I'd ever worked at the resort had me falling into bed in an exhausted heap each evening. I went to sleep early every night, as I had to get up early to get to work at the hotel. After I got off my shift there, it was time to go to the shop and put in a few hours more before heading back to my suite at the hotel for the night.

As hard as it all was, the money I had stacking up in my account made it worth it. Soon I would begin buying things for the baby, and I couldn't wait. I hadn't told a soul about my pregnancy yet. My tummy was barely starting to show just yet. I knew I would have no choice but to tell my employers eventually, but I wanted to keep it to myself for a little bit longer.

Galen may not have ever meant to keep me, but I would always have a part of him. That comforted me. He may not have ever loved me, but I had loved him deeply. I still did, despite his callous attitude and words.

Had it not been for being so tired all the time, I would've been crying over him still. I doubt I would've been able to get much sleep at all either. I was thankful for the hard work as it had kept my mind busy and my body tired.

Heading back into the hotel, I saw the manager behind the reservation desk. He waved at me, signaling me to approach him, so I went. "Afternoon, Mr. Bagwell."

"Come, Ariel, I need to talk to you about something." He turned to walk into his office and I followed, wondering what he could possibly want to speak to me about.

He gestured to the chair in front of his desk, and I sat down as he closed the door behind us. "Have I done something wrong, sir?" Nerves were beginning to sprout inside of me.

"No, not at all, Ariel." He took a seat behind his desk and looked at me with concern in his expression. "We had a man stop by this morning. He asked about you. Would there be any reason someone would be seeking you out?"

My heart sped up. "Sir, did this man have dark hair, blue eyes, and an Irish accent?"

"He did." His expression turned serious.

Fear began to fill me. "Did you tell him anything about me, sir?"

"Of course not." Mr. Bagwell shook his head. "We never tell

strangers anything about our employees. Can I ask you why this man would be looking for you?"

"He and I dated. He said some things that I didn't agree with, and I left him just before coming back here to London." I had no idea that Galen would come this far to look for me.

Those weren't the actions of a man who couldn't love anyone.

Mr. Bagwell looked as if he didn't completely understand. "Do you not want to see this man then?"

"No, I don't want to see him." He might've only been trying to track me down so he could have the privilege of ending things himself. I was sure it would've been a real blow to his ego that I left him instead of the other way around. "Please don't tell him about me if he comes back."

"I won't. And no one else will either. But I must encourage you to deal with this man before he becomes a problem for the hotel. And if you're in any danger, please let me know. We don't want to risk your security here." He tapped the desk with his fingers. "Who is he, anyway? He looks familiar to me."

I internally debated whether I should tell my boss or not, and decided I should. "His name is Galen Dunne. You might recognize him because—"

"Galen Dunne?" he interrupted. "He's filthy rich!" He slammed his hands down on his desk, and he jumped up. "Ariel, you dated that man? And you left him?"

I knew Galen had a pretty stellar reputation with the public—aside from being massively wealthy, he was also known for his philanthropy and down-to-earth attitude. Still, Mr. Bagwell's incredulity had me a little shaken.

Maybe the pregnancy had me feeling a bit more dramatic than normal, but the more his questions sank in, the more they devastated me. "It was...a complicated situation. So, now you know who he is and what he is to me. I need to know that no one will tell him anything about me, not even if he offers them money."

He took his seat as he nodded. "No one will take his money in exchange for information. But you really should deal with the man.

He seemed very persistent, and this could be bad for the hotel if he keeps coming back. He's got plenty of money to get his way—I'm sure you realize that."

I was also sure that he would get bored of tracking me down. "I believe that he'll move on if he doesn't get any information about me soon."

The way he huffed told me he didn't believe that at all. "I should tell you that he told me that you'd misunderstood something he'd said. All he seemed to want was the opportunity to explain himself."

Misunderstood him? How can that be? I'd heard him plain as day.

I doubted there was anything he could say to me that would make me feel better about what I'd overheard that day.

GETTING UP, I knew I had to call Abigail and give her the head's up that he might come looking for me at her shop. "If that's all, I've got to get going, sir. Thank you for the information, and thank you for not telling him anything about me." I went to the door and felt him watching me, so I turned back to look at him. "I've listened to what you've said, and I'll talk to him if he starts to make a scene here. I promise. But if he doesn't, then I want to stay away from him."

"Good enough." He nodded, and I left his office.

Now I felt I had to be very careful. I walked back to the staff elevator and decided to stay off the main floor of the hotel as much as possible. I didn't want Galen coming up on me and starting a fight in public—especially not at my workplace.

As soon as I got into my room, I was racked with sobs and fell on the bed to cry it all out. "Why has he come? Can't he just let me go? He was going to let me go anyway, so why come to torment me now?"

Holding my stomach as I lay on the bed and looked up at the ceiling through tear-filled eyes, I had to ask myself if I'd done the right thing by leaving him. Now he was trying to find me, and what would happen if he did?

If he found out about the baby, what would he do then? Try to take it from me?

I sat up, grabbed a tissue to wipe my eyes and another to blow my nose before calling Abigail to warn her. "Sunny Day Shop, Abigail speaking. How can I help you today?"

"Abigail, it's me, Ariel. Look, I'm not going to be able to work for you for a while. Someone has come looking for me that I don't want to find me. He won't be able to find me while I'm working at the hotel, but I'm worried if I leave then he'll find me in no time."

"Oh, Ariel. There was already a man here asking about you this morning." Her words struck fear in my heart.

"Abigail, what did you tell him?" I clutched the phone so tightly I feared I might break it.

"Nothing, dear. I told him I didn't know an Ariel Pendragon," she said, and I immediately blew out a breath in relief. "He was a smelly older man. Stank like old coffee. I figured he might be some man from your days in the streets that you would have no need for."

I had no idea who that man was. "So, he wasn't a handsome Irishman then?"

"Not at all." She laughed a bit. "There was nothing handsome about him. He just asked if I knew you, and I said no. Then he left. You're not in any danger, are you, dear?"

"No, no. Nothing like what you're thinking." I replied.

The only danger was to my heart and my pride.

CHAPTER 24

Galen

After three weeks with no information and no leads to get closer to finding Ariel, I decided to go to social media to flush her out. Someone would give me information on her, I was sure of it.

The private investigator I'd hired proved nothing more than a drunk who took my money only to purchase as much alcohol as he possibly could. After a few days, he wasn't in any kind of state to help me find Ariel. I'd let him go once I found him in a bar nearly falling off his barstool.

Alone once more, I figured I was the only one up for this task. It was something I had to do on my own. No help needed. I could find one little woman on my own, couldn't I?

Sure, nearly four months had passed since I'd seen Ariel, but I was sure my idea of using social media would end our separation for good. It had to. Her absence had worn badly on me. I had trouble sleeping, eating, and thinking. I was done with all that.

Time for an attitude adjustment—I was done feeling sorry for myself. That was for losers. And I wasn't about to lose in this. I wasn't about to lose my woman.

Tapping away on my laptop, I started the search for my missing girl with a simple post: Looking for one Ariel Pendragon of London. It's urgent that I speak with her.

Attaching a picture of her, I clicked send then let the internet take its turn at tracking down her or anyone who knew her.

I'd made myself a turkey on rye before I'd set to work. Picking it up, I took a bite then waited while I watched the screen. Using my verified account ensured that my audience was beyond the normal size. I had followers from all around the globe—someone would have to know her or know of her.

I picked up the glass of milk I'd poured myself to drink with my sandwich. Looking at the glass, I couldn't recall the last time I'd drank any milk. It had been my go-to drink for a long time. Without Ariel, it seemed I'd forgotten that.

I'd lived my entire life without her or anyone else. To think that she'd embedded herself so deeply in me didn't seem normal. How did I go from needing no one to living my life for someone?

Life made no sense to me. Not since Ariel had entered it. She'd snuck up on me. She had become not just a person I wanted around, but a person I needed to have around. Without her joining me in my life, I would be useless.

A message came up. It asked if I would accept a friend request from Pearl Onion, and there was no picture. The name was certainly bogus, but I accepted the request anyway. Something told me that if Ariel did want to see what I had to say, she wouldn't show up on my social media under her true identity.

A half hour passed without anything significant coming up, and then Pearl Onion made a comment: What would be so urgent that you would search for this Ariel person just to say something to her?

The comment bothered me a bit. At first, I didn't know if I should respond or not. But then I typed a response. Do you know Ariel Pendragon?

No, came very quickly.

So that made my response even easier. Then I have nothing to say to you.

When Pearl Onion made another comment, I began to think the person might actually be Ariel. So quick to cut off communication, are you? I suppose she's not worth the effort anyway.

Feeling baited, I had to ignore the urge to end the session permanently with the stranger. Ariel is worth all the effort in the world to me, but I don't want to waste my time with people who won't help me find her.

There was a long period of silence after I sent that to Pearl. But the comments were anything but silent, with everybody chiming in with their two cents about what I could possibly want with this Ariel person.

When a message from Pearl popped up again, I couldn't help but hear it in Ariel's voice. And why is she worth all this effort?

It was as if she was right there on the other end of the screen. I could almost see her as she sat at her laptop, typing away as she thought about how carefully she had to word things so I didn't find out it was her.

Ariel and I had been seeing each other for a few months last year, but she left me on Christmas. She'd overheard some things that I said, and she'd taken them for the truth when they were anything but that. All I want is the chance to talk to her. In person. I thought adding that at the end would make it clear that I wasn't about to give up on her.

What kinds of things did she overhear you say? Pearl wrote back.

I was ready to admit it all. I've been a confirmed bachelor for a very long time. I was joking with my family about how I intended to stay that way, but I wasn't being truthful with them. It was a mistake. If I could go back to change that, I would.

Ten minutes drifted by without a word from 'Pearl', and that made me even more certain that it was Ariel I was connecting with. When the next thing popped up, I nearly laughed—it sounded so much like my missing girl. If being a free man is so very important to you, why let the girl bog you down?

I replied immediately, knowing exactly what I needed to say. She has never bogged me down. That woman has only served to lift me up. If you know where I can find her to talk to her in person, I could offer you a reward. I knew that would get to Ariel if it were her.

I was right. So now there's a reward for information on this woman who you hurt so badly? Unfair, in my opinion. I could tell she didn't want anything like that to happen. If money were on the line, then I would have tons of leads for her whereabouts.

So I decided to make good on my threat, editing my initial post. Any information that leads to me finding Ariel Pendragon will be rewarded with a million dollars.

Now comments flooded my screen. All of a sudden everyone had an idea about where the woman could be. And some even went so far as to say that they had seen her and would tell me after they were given the money.

I knew I couldn't trust any of them. I wouldn't be wandering around following their leads. But Pearl's silence spoke to me. I'd frightened her with the offer. Pearl, you there? I messaged her.

Nothing came for a while but more comments from people swearing they knew where I could find my missing girl. Then, finally, another response from Pearl. It seems that most of the population would give out information that is not theirs to give for a bit of cash. How terrible.

She was right, and I knew that. I didn't want to upset Ariel if it were her. I think you're right. That was a mistake on part and I'll fix it.

I edited my post again, explaining that I had spoken with a friend who'd pointed out that offering money was not a good idea. I ended the edit with an apology, telling everyone that the reward money was off the table.

People did not respond well. There was a slew of ugly comments directly toward whoever the 'friend' was who told me to rescind the offer.

I hoped that Pearl wasn't paying attention to the comments, but her next message made it clear that she was. Seems I'm the bad guy now. Thanks for that. I've had enough of this.

"No!" I didn't want to lose her.

Trying to figure out how to keep her talking to me, I decided to get as honest as possible. Pearl, I am sorry about that. Pay no mind to my followers. I truly want to talk to Ariel. It's all I think about. I've missed her more than words can express. She was a part of me in a way that can't be replaced. And I made the mistake of not telling her how I felt about her.

I stared at the screen, hoping she would respond again. Thankfully, she did.

It doesn't matter how you felt about her if you never meant to make her a part of your life. I'm sure that one day you would've grown tired of her and left her anyway. I have looked up some facts on you. You've been known to do such things your whole life.

She was right. But that didn't mean that I was the same man. Where do you live? I don't see it on your profile. I began searching through her profile and found it had only been created that day. Who is this, really?

And that was that, Pearl Onion was done talking. She didn't send me any more messages. And that, more than anything, told me that I had been speaking with Ariel. The one thing I knew was that she was definitely watching my social media. But she wouldn't comment on it anymore. She wasn't dumb. And I knew then that she meant to stay hidden from me.

I could've gone back to making the offer of money again and most likely have her brought to me without much ado at all. But I didn't want things to go that way. I'd already messed up once. I wasn't about to do it again.

Going back to my page, I made a new post:

Ariel Pendragon, if you are out there somewhere, I want you to know that I never meant the words you overheard me say. My mission that day was to lead everyone to think that I would never end my bachelor days. I had a surprise I was going to give you that Christmas night at midnight.

I added a picture of the engagement ring to the post before publishing it.

Now she knew that I had an engagement ring. The ball would be in her court. If all she needed was reassurance about my willingness to commit, I figured that should do the trick.

But then my own fears set in. What if she hasn't been thinking about me the same way I've been thinking about her while we've been apart? What if she's gotten over me? What if she thinks she's better off without me?

If she can live without me, then our love wasn't true at all.

All this time, Ariel had thought I was the one who would be incapable of love. But what if it proved to be her? Would I end up alone again? Would I be able to take that?

I prayed I was right about Pearl being Ariel. I prayed Ariel was still looking at her computer screen, reading my words to her. And I prayed that she would believe what I'd written.

So much was at stake. The odds weren't in my favor, and I would have to accept that. Ariel held all the cards right now.

She pretty much always had.

CHAPTER 25

Ariel

I couldn't take my eyes off the gorgeous engagement ring that lit up my computer screen. I couldn't lie to myself and say that it didn't get to me. My heart was pounding, and I could feel tears coming to my eyes.

But is he just playing with my head? If he is, then why? Just to soothe his ego?

Placing my hand on my stomach, I wondered if I should come clean with Galen and tell him that I was actually messaging him as Pearl Onion. When butterflies began to swarm inside my tummy, I decided it was enough of a sign not to tell him.

The hour was late, nearly midnight. When a knock came to my door, I jerked my head to look at it. "Who is it?" My body tensed, thinking it was him.

"It's me, Cherry," came my assistant manager's voice.

Putting on a robe, I covered my scantily clad body to go to the door. I'd begun to sleep in only my panties, as I tossed and turned so much lately that my nightclothes would get bunched up around me, making me uncomfortable.

Since finding out Galen was in London, not even my busy work schedule had been enough to help me sleep. I felt as if he'd find me at every turn and that had me on pins and needles.

Opening the door, I stepped back to allow Cherry to come inside. "What is it that's so important, Cherry?"

"I had to work the nightshift at the front desk tonight, and I've been online. It seems this man you're trying to avoid isn't going to make that easy for you." She held up her cell to show me that she too was on social media. And there was Galen's shout-out to me. "It seems you may have been wrong about this man, and I wanted to make sure you saw this right away."

I went to take a seat on the loveseat in the living area of the suite. "Thanks Cherry, but I've already seen that. And I don't know if I should believe him or not."

She took a seat next to me, giving me a look that said she thought I might be a bit on the crazy side. "Ariel, how can you not believe him? He has a ring, doesn't he? Whatever you heard, he'd just been saying it to throw everyone off his scent so he could surprise you."

Shaking my head, I just couldn't believe that to be true. And if it was, then how could I live with the reality that I had actually been the cause of both of our hurt? "Everything he'd said matched up so well with the man he was when I first met him, though. He'd been very honest with me in the beginning, and I knew Galen wasn't the type of man I should've been with. He had a reputation for dropping women like flies when his mind went elsewhere. I'd deluded myself by thinking he could be with me forever. Once I actually heard him bragging about his bachelorhood to his family and telling them that I was well aware of it all, I couldn't stay. It all felt like a charade, and I couldn't go on with that any longer."

Her eyes glued to mine, she wasn't giving up. Cherry and I had developed a bit of a friendship since I'd started working at the hotel, so I trusted her to be honest with me. "Look, I know it's scary to hand someone your heart and hope he does right by it. But this is going overboard. At least talk to the man. You've been very secretive about your relationship with him. Let me in, Ariel. Let me help you. I doubt you can see this, but everyone else can. You're not happy in the least. You're a shell of a person. You do your work and then you hide away in your suite. It's no life at all. And I can't stand by and watch you do this to yourself any longer. This man is reaching out to you in every way imaginable. Please, just speak to him."

I knew if I saw Galen I would melt into his arms without hesitation. Even hearing his voice over the phone would be too much temptation. Cherry had no idea how much of my heart he held in his hands. I felt I belonged to him as much as I belonged to myself. Carrying his child just made that feeling even stronger.

She held her cell up, showing me the picture of the ring. I nodded. "I saw it. But I don't believe he had that at Christmas. He could've gotten it right here in London. I did see the Tiffany & Co logo engraved on the inside of the ring, you know."

Cherry looked at the picture closer then smiled. "Well, now that we know that, we can do a little detective work."

"I don't see the need for that." Tiffany's was in London, after all.

Cherry wouldn't be stopped though. "Just because we have one here doesn't mean he purchased that ring here. Tiffany's is a huge company, you know. They've got stores all over. Now, where did you say you were at Christmas, Ariel?"

"Portland, Oregon. I doubt there's one there." I'd had no clue that there were any Tiffany's other than the one I'd seen in London. That made me feel a little on the ignorant side. There was so much to learn about the world, and so far I'd learned little. I couldn't help but see a parallel with that and my personal life. I knew so little about men, so little about relationships.

"Ah ha!" Now she sounded like Sherlock Holmes. "There is one in Portland, Oregon. He certainly could've gotten that ring there. Was there ever a time while you two were there that he was gone for a bit?"

I had to think about that. There were a few times he'd left the estate to go do this or that. And he'd gone alone each time. But that didn't matter. "I still don't think he had the ring then. I think he bought it to try to trick me."

"And why would he want to trick you, Ariel?" She rolled her eyes. "You're such a drama queen. I had no idea."

She really did have no idea. "Look, Galen has always been the one in control with women. Relationships end when he's tired of them. It's never been the other way around. I asked him about his other relationships. He doesn't even consider what he's done with other women relationships. And not once did any one of those women walk away from him. He did all the walking."

"Still, I don't see why you think he's trying to dupe you." Cherry really had no clue what powerful people were like. I'd seen my share of bad behavior from the guests on the island.

So, I educated her. "Cherry, think about it. I was a homeless girl from the streets of London. He took me in, gave me a job and security. He quite nearly gave me his heart. He stopped just short of that. And the thing is, I was almost certain that he'd started to love me. I knew I loved him. I still do."

"Then stop being a fool and go get your man." She smiled at me. "What are you waiting for?"

Shaking my head, I could see she still didn't get it. "What if he's just doing this so he can have the upper hand again? What if he thinks I disrespected him by running off after he'd given me so much, and he just wants to get back at me? My heart can't take that. I miss the man so much that I can barely sleep or eat. I have to force myself do those things, and even then, it's not nearly enough. If he dumped me after getting back together, I'm afraid of what will become of me."

The way her eyes went to stare at the floor told me she finally understood me. "Oh, yes, I can see how he might feel a bit of resentment right now. He helps this poor girl, takes her in—even into his bed—and she up and leaves him on Christmas Eve. That does sound bad, doesn't it?"

Nodding, I agreed. "Yes, it does."

"But you can't say that you're done with him, Ariel." She looked at me once more. "You still love him."

"But I don't think he loves me. Not really." I got up and went to open the door. "If you don't mind, Cherry, I need to be alone. Talking about this has opened up the floodgates, and the tears are about to spill."

Cherry got up and came to the door. Suddenly she threw her arms around me, hugging me. "Ariel, I know you've never considered me your friend, but I do care about you. Please let me help you. I hate to see anyone this unhappy."

"Thank you, but I think it will be a while before I can be happy again." I knew I wasn't in the right frame of mind to be anyone's friend. "Perhaps with time, I'll get over him. And then I'll be able to have more normal relationships with people. For now, I'm finding it hard to let myself believe in anyone."

She let me go, nodding as she did. "Ariel, I get it. I do. But I also know that this is as unhealthy as it gets. You have a theory about his intentions that may very well be true, but you have no real reason to think that way. If you're really set on never contacting him again, then you've got to do everything you can to get over this man. And I know this sounds crazy, but talking to him and confronting him about what you think he's doing would be the best thing for you right now. Either you find out you're right and you get to move on for real, or you find out you're wrong."

Perhaps she's right.

I nodded as I closed the door. "Night, Cherry. See you tomorrow."

She put her hand on the door to stop me from closing it. "Promise me that you will think about what I've said."

"I promise." I shut the door, then let the waterworks flow.

Through a blur of tears, I went back to lie in bed. There would be no sleep that night. I knew I would cry the rest of the night away with soft sobs and tons of tears.

My heart ached, and I wanted nothing more than to open my laptop and connect with Galen so badly. A part of me didn't care if he only took me back to break up with me. At least I would have a bit more time with the man who'd grown to be a part of me. And I carried his baby—perhaps he at least deserved to know that.

There was a definite connection between us. So, if he knew we were about to have a baby, would that make him rethink his plan—if he had one?

Even if it did stop his plan, would I want him to stay with me only for the sake of the child?

No, I would not want that.

I wanted his heart. I wanted his love. I wanted Galen, and I wanted him forever.

Galen had a real family. A wonderful family who clearly loved and cared for each other. I had nothing. He'd been the closest thing I'd had to a family since my father died. Mother and I had been lost in the world.

I began to wonder if I could make a family with just my baby and myself. Mother had failed at that. Would I fail, too?

No one deserved that. Especially not a baby who could have Galen's family to call his own. Was staying away from Galen a disservice to our child?

While deep down I knew it was, the most raw and selfish part of me knew that life would be incredibly difficult if Galen was only in my life because of our child.

No, I can't communicate with the man right now.

CHAPTER 26

Galen

My social media had remained quiet for a few days, and I knew I had to up my game. So I came up with another plan. Ariel had to have known that I was in London. I imagined that bit of news had her hiding out even more so than she had been before.

I made my rounds to the places I was pretty sure she might be working at and gave one last attempt to find out anything about her. And I would let them know that I would be leaving London to return to Portland within the next few days. This news would definitely get back to Ariel, and then she would start coming out of hiding.

Or so I hoped.

I started at The Jumeirah Carlton Tower Hotel. The people I'd come in contact with at that hotel had acted so differently from anyone else I'd talked to that I was pretty sure she was employed there.

Even as I walked up to the front desk, I noticed the lady behind it rushing to knock on the door behind her. "Sir, it's him again."

The man I'd spoken with before came out, and the girl went into the office. He greeted me nicely, "Good morning, sir. How can I be of service to you?"

"Sir, I am Galen Dunne. I've been here before seeking Ariel Pendragon. Are you sure she doesn't work here?" I knew the answer I would get, but I was okay with that.

"Mr. Dunne, as I've told you before, we can't give any information on anyone." He looked off to one side, and for a moment I thought he might be about to tell me something under his breath. But then he looked back at me, staring straight into my eyes. "It's been a bit long for you to still be looking for someone who clearly doesn't want you to find her, don't you think?"

Nodding, I agreed with him, much to his surprise. "Yes, I think it has been going on for too long. Four months is a long time to search someone out. The fact that she's chosen to stay hidden is telling. I guess she'll never give me the chance to make things right with her. I'm leaving London tomorrow morning; I just wanted one last chance to see her. If you do know the woman, it would be nice if you relayed that information to her."

He only shook his head. "Again, sir, I cannot tell you a thing about anyone."

I knew that would be his response, but I hoped the information would still get back to Ariel. "It's okay. Goodbye." I left my business card on the desk, knowing there was a chance he'd get on the phone with Ariel to tell her I would be leaving London the following day. At least he had my number to give to her.

After making visits to the other places I thought she might work at, I set to work on my next plan. I spent the rest of the day renting out some advertising space for a big event I would start in the morning.

When I got back to my hotel room, I called my mother. "Hello?" she answered the call.

"Ma, it's me, Galen. I'm calling because I don't want you hearing about this on the news of any of your gossip shows." I played with the engagement ring I'd pulled from its box. "Tomorrow morning, here in London, I'll be doing a bit of advertising to Ariel. And with that, there will be a proposal of marriage. I'm sure the paparazzi will take quick hold of that and run with it."

"A proposal, Galen?" she asked with surprise. "Are ya sure ya want to go and propose marriage to a woman who left you so easily?"

It might've seemed easy to everyone in my family, but I knew Ariel's heart had been shattered by what I'd said. "She did not leave me easily, Ma, I can assure you of that. She loved me. I know I shattered her heart when she heard me talking to the lads. She's hiding somewhere here in London, nursing her wounds, I'm sure of it."

"But marriage, son? I don't see the rush for that." Ma still didn't understand things.

"Ariel knows so much about my past with women," I began my lament. "She told me from the start that she wanted something more, but I convinced her to compromise. I'm not sure that she's certain I'm genuine in my intentions. In fact, I think she thinks that getting back together is a matter of pride for me. I need to show her otherwise. And besides, the proposal isn't just to get her back—I was going to do it on Christmas Eve anyway. I still love her and still want to spend the rest of my life with her."

"Even though she left you with hardly a backward glance? You still want to marry Ariel?" She huffed, sounding a bit angry about that. "Galen, I don't know."

I knew how much Ariel liked my mother, and if she did accept my proposal only to come home with me to a family who now didn't like her, it would destroy her even further. "Ma, I need you to not hold this against Ariel. She's had a hard life. I can understand why she did this, and I hope that you can see things from her perspective, too. And you need to know that she thought the world of you. If you're against our marriage, it will make her very sad, and she might call the whole thing off."

That was met with a few moments of silence as my mother took it all in. "Well, I suppose I can understand why she did this. If she's thinking you're a vindictive man—though I do think she should know better—then she must be terrified of what you'll do if you get her back. I can see that now. If she accepts your proposal, she will be welcomed here with open arms by us all. I'll talk to the rest of the family and get them to see things for what they are."

"Thank you." I knew I could count on my mother to set things right with my family. "So, I'll be taking over Piccadilly Circus tomorrow for the day. Or longer, if Ariel doesn't react right away. There will be no other ads but mine covering that place, starting at seven in the morning."

My mother laughed. "How unconventional of you, Galen. But then again, I've never known you to do anything the conventional way. Good luck, son. I'll take care of things here. You get your girl. I love you. Bye now."

"I love you, too. Goodbye, Ma." I ended the call then looked at my computer. The videos I'd shot earlier that day had been e-mailed to me.

Opening the file, I watched myself as I got down on one knee, the black box in my hand, exposing the ring inside. I'd donned an Armani tux and had let a stylist fix me up perfectly. By the next afternoon, I was pretty sure most of the world would be seeing this; I knew I had to look great.

That night I found sleep more easily than I had since she'd left me. I dreamt that she would say yes after seeing the big screens in Piccadilly Circus with her name all over them and me on one knee, asking for her hand in marriage.

When I woke, I thought that I'd been a bit deceptive in the ad. I'd said I had left her a ticket at the airport, so she could come to me Portland with me. She would have no idea that I hadn't actually left at all. She would come out into the open. Then I would have my chance.

Though my dreams had been optimistic, I was pretty certain that there was no way she would say yes. Not at that time, anyway.

If Ariel honestly thought I was out to disgrace her for what she'd done, then there would be no way she would fly to me to say yes. But I didn't need her to do that.

This was a trick. The only trick I would play on her. After what happened at Christmas, I was done with tricks. This was just so I could flush her out of hiding.

All I had to do was sit back, watch, and wait.

My eyes were on the Jumeirah Carlton Tower Hotel first and foremost. In the morning, before the billboards blazed at seven a.m., I would be sitting in their breakfast room, waiting.

From that room, I would be able to see the front desk. I was sure, once the news got out, that I would see someone from that desk flocking to Ariel to ask her if she'd heard the news.

To see Ariel again seemed almost too good to be true. I'd missed her for what seemed like an eternity. To hold her in my arms seemed like a far-fetched fantasy. To tell her that I loved her and wanted to make her mine forever seemed like a dream.

But along with all that disbelief came a stream of optimism. There was love between us. Although unspoken, it had grown inside us both. I knew that for sure.

If Ariel hadn't been in love with me when she'd overheard my words, she wouldn't have run. Nothing I said would've hurt her so deeply that she felt she had to leave me if there was no love in her heart for me.

I didn't think I could take one more night without her. I was worried about what would become of me the next day if I had to keep living this way. The time had come to end this thing.

I doubted either of us could take much more anyway. She had to be just as miserable as I. Her nights had to be as sleepless as mine were. She had to miss me holding her all night long after we'd made passionate love.

I'd never made love to anyone but her. Sure, I'd had sex with plenty of women, but that didn't even compare to what I'd shared with Ariel. She'd brought out this romantic man—a man I had no idea existed within me. I wasn't about to let that chap go away. He was a great guy. Even better than the one who'd come before him.

Laughing at myself, I closed my eyes, hoping to go back to sleep for a few hours. The morning would come soon enough, and I had much to do.

When my alarm went off, I got up. After showering, I put on my disguise. A baseball cap, old jeans, a gray t-shirt, running shoes, and a pair of eyeglasses I'd picked up at a thrift shop. A fake beard and a blonde wig finished off my look.

No one at the hotel would know it was me. Even Ariel would find it difficult to see me through all of that stuff.

I threw on a jacket just before heading out of my suite. No one looked twice at me as I left my hotel then walked down the street to where I was almost positive my beloved Ariel was residing.

Going into the breakfast room, I got myself a bagel and some milk then took a seat, making sure I could see the front desk. And there was the manager of the fine establishment. He'd given no mind to me as I entered. If I could fool him, then I could fool the rest of them.

Time's up, Ariel Pendragon. I'm here for you now.

27

CHAPTER 27

Ariel

With it being my day off, I'd planned to sleep in after a rough night of worrying about the sonogram I had scheduled the next day. Well, worry wasn't exactly all I was doing. I also thought about seeing my baby for the first time and the kinds of emotions that would stir in me—excitement being the main one.

Once again, I thought about how much nicer it would be if Galen were there with me to see the baby for the first time. But I knew I couldn't tell him. Not yet. Maybe not ever.

The appointment wasn't until two in the afternoon, so I had lots of time to get ready. Sleep came easier to me in the early morning hours anyway for some reason.

All of the conflict with Galen had me dreaming about the man more than usual.

In my dream, he and I were laying in his bed at his bungalow. The water lapped around the poles under the home as he kissed the side of my neck and lay behind me, spooning me the way he'd always done. "I think tomorrow we'll take a ride on my yacht to check out the surrounding waters. You game?"

Turning in his arms to face him, I placed my palms on either side of his handsome face. "I am. I'd go anywhere with you, babe." I moved in to take his soft lips, parting mine so he could run his tongue in to play with mine.

Our naked bodies inched toward the other's until we were flush against one another. His cock began to pulse to life as we kissed. Eager to accommodate him, I moved my body against his until his erection stabbed against my stomach. He rolled onto his back, pulling me to sit on top of him. Lifting me up, he slid me down his long, hard cock as I moaned with pleasure.

"God, you're beautiful, Ariel." He watched me as I rode him. His hands moved to cup my breasts. "Will I ever get tired of these magnificent tits?"

"I sure hope not." I pulled up one of his hands to suck on his middle finger, pretending it was his manhood.

I adored the way his eyes closed as he let himself go. "Baby, you feel so good, I want you with me forever."

I moved his finger out of my mouth just long enough to say, "You will have me forever. It was in our vows, silly," I pulled the next finger into my mouth to give it some attention.

"Oh, yes. I forgot about that." He chuckled a bit, and his body shook, making me bounce a bit more as I moved up and down his cock. "I still can't believe you actually married me. I was so afraid you wouldn't actually go through with it. I kept thinking, as you were walking down the aisle to me, that you would wink, tell me to go fuck myself, then turn and run away from me."

"Never." I put my hands on his chest then switched my rhythm to give him as much pleasure as I possibly could.

He took me by my arms, looking at me with such intensity. "After what we've gone through, you have to know that I absolutely thought that was possible."

Looking at him with curiosity, I asked, "What are you talking about, Galen? What have we gone through?"

His handsome face wore a puzzled expression. "You left me. Don't you remember that?"

Shaking my head, I laughed. "Galen, you must've been dreaming. I would never leave you. I love you, babe."

"No, you did." He held my arms tighter, stopping all my movement. "You've got to remember that, Ariel. You left me."

"I wouldn't do that." He made me feel as if I'd gone a bit crazy. "Galen, stop. You're freaking me out."

"I'm freaking you out?" Shaking his head, he went on, "Ariel, are you okay?"

As I stared down at him, his face began to blend into the white pillowcase. "Where're you going, Galen?"

"You left me, so I'm leaving you now." He faded away even more. "It's only fair, Ariel."

His hands still held my arms so tightly that I couldn't move, yet his body kept fading away. "No, come back. I don't remember leaving you. Why would I ever leave you? I love you. I love us. I love being your wife, Galen. Don't leave me. Please, don't leave me!"

"It's only fair," his voice sounded as if it came from very far away. "Goodbye, Ariel. That's more than I got from you."

THE SOUND of someone pounding on a door had me opening my eyes, which were filled with tears. I shook my head to try to wipe the webs of the horrible dream away. "It was just a dream." I sat up, wiping my eyes with the back of my hand. "What a terrible dream."

The pounding continued even though I was fully awake. Then I heard a man's voice, "Ariel, wake up. We need to tell you something."

It sounded like my boss, Mr. Bagwell. "Give me a second."

Staggering to the bathroom, I splashed my face with cold water to clean the tears away. I brushed my teeth very quickly then looked at the shower. But the sound of more knocking on the door reminded me that I had company, and they seemed to have run out of patience.

I picked up my robe and put it on as I hadn't managed to dress. Making sure my tits, which were already swelling with the pregnancy, were tucked away, I tied the robe shut then went to the door. "What's going on?"

Right behind Mr. Bagwell was Cherry. Both came into my suite, and Cherry took my hand, pulling me to sit on the loveseat in the living area. "You will never believe this, Ariel!"

With the robe on and no apron to cover my slightly swollen belly, I found Mr. Bagwell eyeing my tummy. "Ariel, there's something you should see." His eyes came up to mine as he held out his cell phone.

I saw lots of billboards and lights and immediately recognized the place that had been my home for nearly three years. "Piccadilly Circus?"

"Look at the signs, Ariel," Cherry coached me. "What do you see?"

All of the billboards will filled with the same image—a man on one knee. "Funny how there's only one advertisement, huh? I guess some company has a big promotion coming up. Can I ask why you two thought I'd want to be woken up for this?" I looked back and forth at them.

Mr. Bagwell sighed, looking over to Cherry. "The picture is too small. She can't make him out." He looked around the room. "Do you have a computer, Ariel?"

"I do, but why do you want it?" I was getting a bit aggravated by their antics. "I've got a lot on my plate today. Being woken up over some silly ad campaign isn't welcome, you guys."

"Tell him where the laptop is, Ariel," Cherry spurred me on. "You'll see once you've got a bigger screen." Her eyes went to my bulging belly and she leaned closer to me, within whispering distance. "Ariel, is there anything you'd like to tell me? I won't tell a soul."

Felling a bit prickly about her question, I called out to Mr. Bagwell, "My laptop is just inside the top drawer of the desk there, sir."

He went to get it as Cherry took my face between her hands. "Ariel Pendragon, I happen to have witnessed that you eat very little, yet your tummy is bulging. Is there a reason for that?"

Pulling her hands from my face, I took a deep breath. "I was going to tell you later this afternoon, after I had a picture of the sonogram to show you both."

Mr. Bagwell stopped in his tracks with my laptop in hand. "Sonogram? Isn't that something a pregnant woman gets?"

I nodded. "Mostly, yes."

His jaw dropped. "You're pregnant?"

Again, I nodded. "I wanted to wait to tell anyone until I had confirmation. I wasn't deliberately trying to hide anything." I had been, but didn't really want to explain why that was.

If anyone had known that I carried Galen Dunne's baby, then things might've gone a lot worse for me than they had. And that fact became apparent as Mr. Bagwell said, "If this baby belongs to Galen Dunne, then you must inform him of that as soon as possible, Ariel." He typed something on my computer then handed it to me.

My heart stopped as I saw the webcam that covered Piccadilly Circus in real time. Galen Dunne covered the entire place. On one knee, a black box with the same shiny diamond engagement ring he'd put on the internet in his hand, he looked out, seemingly at me. "Ariel, I know you're out there. I know you're hurting. But I didn't mean any of it. Ariel, I want you to come back to Portland to marry me. I've left a ticket for you at Heathrow airport. Come to me if you'll accept my proposal. I love you, baby, and I always have. Please, come home and marry me and make me the happiest man in the world."

Closing the laptop, I felt tears burning the backs of my eyes. "Leave me, please."

I had no idea what I would do. Could I even believe the man?

Mr. Bagwell wasn't going to be easily put off. "Ariel, now listen to me. You will tell Mr. Dunne about this pregnancy or I will. It's not fair to hide that kind of knowledge from a man."

Now I found myself in deep trouble. "Please, don't put me on the spot like this, sir."

"I'm afraid I've got to." He shook his head, looking more than a little peeved at me. "You tell the man or I will. If you don't tell him today, I will call him tomorrow morning." He pulled something out of his pocket and handed it to me. "He left his card yesterday when he came by to give me one last chance to tell him where you were. That man deserves to know he has a child, and this child deserves to have his father."

"I don't know if he'll even want this baby," I protested.

"Well, he certainly wants you to be his wife, so I'm pretty sure he'd love to have a child with you. Nevertheless, he will know about this baby from one of us, and very soon." He opened the door, and he and Cherry made a quick exit as I stood still, holding Galen's business card in my hand, wondering what the hell I should do.

Before the door closed all the way, I saw a hand shoot inside to grab it. Someone pushed it back open and then stepped inside, closing it behind him.

"No!" I had no idea who this man was who'd entered my room. Fear took over me as I looked around for something to defend myself with.

"Hush, baby. It's me."

His voice took me by surprise.

Galen?

28

CHAPTER 28

Galen

Her curls were in disarray, yet she still looked gorgeous as her emerald eyes darted around the room, to find something to pummel me with I supposed, as she thought me an intruder. Which, technically I was. "Hush, baby. It's me."

With a sudden jerk, her head pivoted to look at me. At first she said nothing, her eyes scanning my body down, then back up. Her eyes met mine. "You've found me."

Taking off the cap, the wig, the glasses, then the fake beard, I looked at her. "I've found you."

She wrapped her arms around herself, covering her white robe. "I saw your display."

"Good." I couldn't seem to make myself go to her. There was much to be resolved between us before I let myself touch her. If she pushed me away this time, then it would really be over. "I only did that to flush you out, just so you know."

Her eyes went to the floor. "I should've known that."

I had so many questions but had a hard time finding where to start. "How have you been?"

"Not great." She glanced at me sideways. "This hasn't been easy."

"I haven't been great either." A part of me wanted to put the talking away and get to the making up. But my brain needed more. "Ariel, I know what you overheard that day. And I also know that you've heard that it wasn't true. You know that I only said that to throw my family off before I proposed to you later that night. Knowing all that, why would you still hide from me?"

She looked over her shoulder at the sofa. "Care if I take a seat?"

"It's your place," I reminded her. "Do whatever you want."

She sat down, then picked up a throw pillow and held it on her lap, covering herself. I supposed she felt exposed in only the robe. "I couldn't trust that you meant it. I think you're only out here to get me back so you can dump me. I figured I must have bruised your ego something fierce for you to search me out, and figured you wanted to be the one to do the dumping."

I knew it, but hearing her say it actually hurt more than I knew it would. Moving to take a seat on the only other chair in the small sitting area, I asked, "Do you really think that little of me, Ariel?" That had bothered me from the moment she'd left me. "How could you even believe what you heard me telling my brother and in-laws? You knew me. You knew me better than I'd ever let anyone know me. And yet you left so quickly. You didn't even give me a chance to explain myself to you."

"And you think that was unfair of me?" she asked with narrowed eyes. "You think it was unfair of me to leave without giving you a chance to explain. And now you just want to explain yourself and then walk out of my life on your own terms." She looked down. "Go ahead. Explain all you want. Let's just get this over with."

"I have no plans to leave you, Ariel. Whatever you've cooked up in your head isn't true. I did mean the words I said. I do love you." It felt good to get the truth out in the open.

But as good as I felt, Ariel didn't seem to feel that way. "Galen, why would you still love me? If you never meant for me to overhear those words, and I left you without giving you so much as a goodbye, why would you still love me?"

I seemed to be the only person in the world who knew that answer. "Ariel, I loved you then. I love you now. Yes, it hurt like hell that you left without giving me a chance to say anything to you. Yes, I felt so much anger at you for a long time. But then it ebbed, and what was left was empathy. I could feel your pain. You'd always had an underlying fear that I would grow tired of you. Or that I would find something else to take my attention away from you."

She nodded as she looked at the floor with unblinking eyes. "Yes, that was always there. You're right. But did I have the right to leave you without giving you a chance?"

"In a way, you did." As much as I'd been hurt by her leaving, I had to accept my role in it. "Ariel, I should've told you that I loved you when I first felt it. That had been part of our deal. I should've been open with you with each new thing I found out about myself. I found out I needed you, and yet I didn't tell you that. I found out that I wanted to live my life with you, but again, I waited a bit too long to let you know about that."

"That doesn't seem so unusual," she said quietly. "I see that now. But instead of speaking to you about how our feelings were progressing, I heard some hurtful things and ran off like a dumb kid." She looked at me. "I've realized that about myself, Galen. I'm ignorant in a lot of ways. You deserve more."

"You're not ignorant, Ariel. Don't say things like that. You're just young." I hated that she seemed to be second guessing herself in so many ways.

The way she looked at me with pure bewilderment made me smile at her. She smiled back, and my heart leapt. "I've got a question for you," she whispered.

"Go ahead." I was eager to get her participation in our conversation, and was ready to answer anything she had to ask.

"Why me, Galen? Why a poor girl from the streets of London?" She kept holding my eyes with her own. "Is it because I'm young and you can mold me to your liking? Or is it that I don't threaten you in any way? You know, like you will always have the upper hand because you're so much older and wiser than I am?"

"Upper hand? Me?" The girl had no idea of her hold on me. "Baby, you've got it all. You hold all the cards, and you always have. The fact that you think I even want the upper hand tells me that you've been sitting here in this place, making up things in your head about our relationship. But here's the truth for you: you and I simply worked in a way that we've never worked with anyone else in our lives."

"How am I to believe you?" She looked away again. "How am I to believe that you will never find something you find more important than me?"

"Well, nothing's cropped up that's been more important to me in the last four months. Or even all those months before that, when we were together." I thought I should be as open and honest as I could be with her. "You are my world, Ariel. I know that I was alive before I met you, but now I can't imagine living without you. I can't remember who I even was before I found you."

Blinking, she shook her head. "No, that can't be. You're the great Galen Dunne. You've accomplished so much. You're just trying to make me feel better."

"I am not. I'm not being even the slightest bit dishonest." I got up and went to sit on the other end of the sofa, needing to be closer, but knowing better than to get any closer than that just yet. I didn't want her to feel rushed.

"So you, a man with so much going on in his life, doesn't know who he is without me?" She smiled at me. "And you want me to believe that?"

"I expect you should." I thought I should point out a few things to her. "You see, I haven't done one thing but spend time with you since I brought you to the island. And after you left, I didn't do a thing but look for you. People have called, asking me to do this or that." I shook my head. "But I turned them all down. And I let them know that I had to find my other half before I could ever expect to be able to think clearly again."

Her laughter pealed through the air, and it made my heart sing to hear it again. "Galen Dunne, you are messing with me."

"I am not." Maybe she needed to know some more about what I'd put off for her. "A man from Spain called to ask me to come in on something he's working on. It's an engine he claims can run on air. Can you believe that? If it works, it's miraculous how much that could change the entire planet. And I told him I couldn't get back to him about that until I found you. And do you know what he said to me about that, Ariel?"

"How could I know that?" She grinned.

I had to tell myself to take a breath, as she'd stolen it with that grin. "Ariel, he told me that he'd lost a love once. When he finally got her to come back to him, it was too late. She had advanced cancer and succumbed to it only a year after their marriage. He told me not to give up until I had you back. His invention could wait for that."

"How thoughtful of him." With a tilt of her head, she asked, "So, tell me what it is you really want from all this, Galen."

There it was—my chance. "Ariel, I want you in my life. Not for a little while and not on my terms. I want you to be my other half. And I want to be the other half of you, too. I never want to leave you behind."

"But the proposal is off?" she asked with a smile on her face, which I found odd.

"I'd like to give you a much better one if you would like to give me the chance to do that. The billboard thing isn't exactly romantic." At least I hadn't thought it was.

"You've got to be kidding me, Galen. That's the most romantic thing I've ever heard of." She stood up and walked to stand directly in front of me, her arms crossed over her midsection. "Before you go and ask me to marry you, you should know a little bit more about me."

I thought I knew pretty much everything there was to know. "I don't know what you could possibly say that would make me change my mind about living the rest of my life with you, but go ahead."

"We'll see." She moved her hands to the belt of the robe.

I thought she might have gotten a tattoo or something that she thought might put me off. "I assure you, there is nothing about you that will stop me from loving you and wanting to share our lives together."

Slowly, she pulled the belt until it fell away, allowing the robe to gape open in front. She was only wearing panties and my cock immediately took notice. But my eyes followed as she ran her hands over her round belly—a belly that was much rounder than it had been before. She moved one hand up to one of her big tits, which also looked even bigger than it had before. Then she asked, "Notice anything different about me, Galen?"

No way!

CHAPTER 29

Ariel

Although nearly naked in front of the man I'd been cursing for the past four months, I felt no shame at all. His child, which was cuddled in my womb, made him a part of me, and that could never be changed. "Notice anything different about me, Galen?"

His blue eyes scanned my body, lingering on my stomach, then my breasts. I held my breath as he took his time coming up with an answer. Slowly, his eyes came up to meet mine. "Before I say anything else, I'd like to ask you a question."

"Okay." I felt that was only fair, but I held my breath as nerves settled in my stomach.

His expression turned stoic. "Do you love me, Ariel Pendragon?"

"I do." It felt good to say it.

But apparently he needed to really hear me say it. "Ariel, can you say it then?"

"I love you, Galen Dunne." I rubbed my belly. "Care to answer my question now? Do you notice anything unusual about my body?"

He scratched his brow as he his lips pulled into a smile. "I do believe that you've got yourself a bun in the oven."

"You're right. It's been baking for about four months now." I pulled my robe closed again. "Our methods of birth control failed, I'm afraid."

Going to his knees in front of me, Galen pulled my robe open again then pressed his lips to my belly as he cradled it in his hands. "Ariel, you're having our baby." He looked up at me with glistening eyes. "I think I'm supposed to be mad at you for not telling me this. But I'm so damn happy that I can't seem to muster any anger at all."

He's happy!

That was all I needed to hear. I reached down to run my fingers through his thick dark hair. "Galen, you have no idea how wonderful it is to hear you say that. My God, I love you."

"Can we kiss and make up now?" he asked me.

All I could do was nod as a lump filled my throat. He rose in front of me, running his hands up my body as he did. His touch spread like lightning through me.

Picking me up in his strong arms, my feet left the floor as he pulled me up so we were eye-to-eye, then he placed his lips on mine. For a moment I thought I was back in my dream.

The warmth of his breath as it moved into my mouth let me know it was real. The way he held me so close left no doubt that he was real, and he was right there with me.

Going back to his knees, he laid me on the floor then pulled my robe all the way off. His hands ran over my tits then my stomach before he took my panties off with one ripping motion.

I shuddered with a chill as he stood up, taking his clothes off in record time. Naked, he looked at his jeans that lay in a heap on the floor. He reached down to pick them up then pulled the black box out of the pocket. "I want to do this now."

Sitting up, I felt my entire body quivering. "You do?"

He nodded. "I do." Galen got on one knee in front of me. "Ariel, I've never loved anyone the way I love you. I won't always do or say the right things. I won't always be the man you deserve. But I'm sure going to try. Marry me, my darling, bear my children, and live this life with me until there's no more to live."

"Now, that was beautiful." I held out my left hand, wiggling my ring finger at him. "I will marry you, Galen. I have loved you for a long time, and nothing would make me happier than to give you as many children as you want. And living with you at my side is the only way I would ever want to live. You hold my heart, and I think you always have."

His hand shook as he slipped that ring on my finger. "Thank you, my love. I'll make sure you never regret any of this."

"I'll make sure you don't regret this either. We're a team, you and I." I looked at the shining ring and then at my fiancé.

The way he gazed at me stopped my heart. "You're mine, and I am yours." He leaned forward, pressing his lips to mine as he laid me back on the carpeted floor once more.

We both made horrible sounds of relief as he thrust into me. I ran my foot along the back of his leg, looking at him when he pulled his lips from mine to stare into my eyes. Moving my hands to hold his face, I whispered, "I've never been happier than this moment right here. Thank you for hunting me down. And thank you for never giving up on our love."

Galen looked as if he might cry. He kissed me instead, taking us higher and higher. Our bodies glided together, moving in ways that they hadn't in far too long.

My insides quivered with my first orgasm, and he groaned as I came all over him. His dick jerked and twitched before he abruptly pulled out of me. "Shit, I nearly lost it."

I looked at him with a smile on my face. "Go ahead and lose it, silly. I'm already pregnant."

"Oh, shit." His face turned a shade of pink. I'd never seen him embarrassed before.

"You look so cute." I arched my body up and he moved back into me. "We don't have to worry about anything for now."

"God, this feels great. All the sex we want, and no worries because we've already made a little person." He laughed as he moved with more vigor. "We're having a baby, Ariel! You and me!" He kissed me again.

I wrapped my arms around his neck, moving with him. Once he ended the kiss, I let him know a little more good news. "I've got an appointment later today. They're going to do a sonogram. We'll get to know the sex of the baby today."

"No way!" The smile he wore was off the charts. "What a day. I've got myself a fiancé, a baby on the way, and I get to be there when I find out what we're having. My family is going to be in for a surprise."

"Seems you get to surprise them after all." I was glad he was getting some of what he'd wanted.

His laughter made my heart pound—it was so good to hear again. All I wanted was happiness for us both for the rest of our lives. And I would do all I could to make sure that happened.

I had no idea if it was the time apart, the makeup sex, or the incredible mood we were in, but when the next orgasm hit me, I just about passed out. And by the sounds Galen made, he was feeling pretty similarly.

Huffing and puffing, we lay there on the carpet, soaked in sweat and saturated in love. "I love you, Ariel."

"I love you, too, Galen." And I knew I always would.

After a shower and a nap, he and I got up and got ready to learn what sex our baby was. But what we found when we went outside was the last thing either of us expected.

There were cameras everywhere. Somehow the press had found out where we were. Questions flew at us both, but Galen handled them well. "Yes, I've found her. And yes, she's accepted my proposal."

The cheers that came up from all who surrounded us surprised me. "Glad you all approve."

I saw Abigail's face in the crowd, and I moved toward her as she shouted, "Congratulations, Ariel!"

"Thank you, Abigail." I reached out to hug her. "I'll be by tomorrow to fill you in. For now, just know that you need to hire someone to replace me permanently."

"I'm so happy for you." She let me go as Galen pulled me to go with him.

Waving at her, I felt like things were going to be okay now. Like forever okay, not just for a little while. My hard times were over, a thing of the past.

Soon I would be Mrs. Galen Dunne. I would be the wife of a billionaire. My children would never have to worry about living the kind of life I had. And I had Galen to thank for that. And I knew we'd raise our children to make sure they would never be helpless. Money could disappear, but perseverance and conviction could get you through anything.

We slipped into the backseat of a cab, and Galen kissed my cheek. "Wow, what a turnout, huh?"

"Galen, you're my hero. I want you to know that." I kissed his cheek. "I truly don't know what I did to deserve you, but I'm glad I've got you."

"Well then, you should know that you're my hero, too. I never would've known love if it weren't for you." He ran his arms around my shoulders and held me close. "This feels perfect."

It did feel right. Everything did. Even lying on a table with cold jelly all over my tummy. A woman ran a round thing over my stomach as Galen and I watched the screen for any signs of life within my womb.

"Well, no wonder," the woman said. "I saw your chart, and when I weighed you, I wondered why you'd gained so much weight since the last time you were here."

I looked up at Galen. "I suppose I've been eating too much. Funny, I thought I wasn't eating enough. I've been forcing myself to eat since I had no appetite. I suppose I'd better slow down."

The woman laughed. "No. It's not because you've been eating too much." She pointed to the screen. "Can you see those two things moving?"

Galen leaned in close. "Well, I see something moving."

I, too, stared at the black and white screen. "Care to tell me what we're looking at, ma'am?"

"Two hearts." She pointed them out and then they came into perfect view.

"Oh," I said. Then I thought about what that meant. "Oh..."

Galen clapped me on the shoulder. "Way to go, Momma. You're going for two at a time, it seems. So what do we have there, Doc?"

The woman looked at him. "Oh, I'm not the doctor. I'm a sonographer."

"Okay," Galen said with a smile. "So, what are we having, sonographer?"

She moved the thing over my stomach some more, then smiled. "Well, here's a little boy."

I gasped as I looked at Galen for his reaction. And I was in tears as he smiled at me. "You're giving me a son, baby." He kissed me on the forehead. "I can't wait to meet him."

The sonographer gave us more news, "And this one is a girl."

"One of each," I said, then started to really cry.

Galen kissed my tears away. "You've given me the world and then some, baby."

"You've done the same for me, too, Galen." I sobbed, feeling so happy that things had all worked out before I got this news. "If I'd have been alone, I would've been a mess right now."

The lady handed me some tissues, then used a few to clean the jelly off my belly. "Yeah, would've been," she joked.

She may have thought me a mess then, but if I'd been on my own —if Galen and I hadn't made up—boy, would I have been a wreck.

It seems someone up there really likes me.

CHAPTER 30

Galen

The sun shone down on us as Ariel and I entered my family home in Portland. My family knew about me and Ariel before I was able to tell them a thing. The news had announced our impending nuptials to the world.

We had a lot more surprises to give my family though. "Are you ready for the onslaught, my love?" I kissed Ariel on the forehead as she stood in front of the door.

"I don't know." She looked at the ring on her finger. "We're pregnant before the marriage, Galen. What if your parents don't approve?"

"Nonsense." I reached around her to open the door, as we'd come home unexpectedly.

One of the maids gasped as we walked in. "Oh, my goodness. Your mother will be speechless."

I winked at her. "Oh, you have no idea."

Taking Ariel by the hand, I led her up the stairs to our wing. We had some things to do before seeing anyone. "Galen, don't surprise your mother too much. We don't want to give her a heart attack."

"I'll be careful." As we topped the stairs, we found my family had a surprise for us as well. A sign that said, 'Welcome Home, Newlyweds!' hung above the top of the stairs. "Well, they certainly have assumed a lot, now haven't they?"

"Oh, now I feel really bad about telling them our big news." Ariel frowned. "Maybe we should lie and tell them we are married, and then tell them about the babies."

"No way." Ariel and I had made plans for a large wedding with lots of guests, and we wanted each one of my nieces and nephews to be in it, too. They weren't going to take that away from us just because they'd assumed we'd married before coming home.

When I opened the bedroom door, we got another surprise. "Oh my God." Ariel looked back at me, and I could feel my jaw drop.

There was a small bassinet at the foot of the bed. And a banner hung from one of the corner of the bedpost to the other. This banner read, 'Now get to making babies!'

"I am so sorry." I shook my head as I lead Ariel into the room, closing the door behind us. "But you should look on the bright side. They definitely want us to give them some grandkids ASAP."

Ariel and I peered into the bassinet, finding it filled with newborn diapers, bottles, and tiny blankets. Ariel picked up a blanket, rubbing it along her cheek. "So soft. Well, at least we've got a start to all the things we're going to need. I think our news might be welcome after all. But we'll have to hurry up on the wedding. I know I've said I want to wait until after the birth so I could wear something more flattering, but I think a dress that's very full at the bottom will look good too."

"You'll look great in anything." I picked her up, spinning around with her. "And we can get married as soon as you'd like, too."

A smile lit her face. "At the resort, Galen! Can we do it there?"

"Anywhere, anytime—you're the boss on that front." I gave her a kiss, then put her feet back on the floor. "Now, let's get changed then go tell my parents our news."

I'd had the rest of Ariel's things that were left on the island sent to Portland. When she opened her closet, she just about fainted. "You got my clothes here?"

"My plan was always to bring you home. So of course I had your things sent here." I watched her as she ran her hands over the dresses she'd bought with her own money.

"I thought I'd lost all I'd worked for." She turned to look at me. "Thank you."

"Look in the top drawer in there." I'd had something made for her and was pretty sure she would love it.

I went in behind her so I could see her reaction. She pulled the drawer open and found the one item that was in there. A black leather album.

She smiled at me, glancing at me over her shoulder as I moved in behind her to hold her by the waist. "What have you done?"

"Something I loved doing." I kissed the side of her neck.

She opened the front cover, and there was an eight by ten of one of the many photos she'd taken on the island. "See, I told you that you had a natural talent." The sun's rays rippled on the waves outside my bungalow on the island, the picture perfectly capturing the view. "I took the SD card out of the camera to make this for you before you left. Did you ever notice it missing?"

She shook her head as she turned the page to find a sunrise that focused on one seabird as pinks and blues filled the space around it. "No, I never felt like taking any pictures. I didn't even take one."

"Well, you've got to start taking pictures again. You really do have a gift for it." I leaned my chin on her shoulder as I held her and looked at each picture with her.

When she turned the page, there was one of the many pictures she'd taken of me without my knowledge. "Oh, lord. Seems you caught me." She laughed. "You must think I'm some kind of stalker."

"If you're one, then I'm one, too." That was no joke. If I'd have told a soul about everything I'd done to find my girl, then I would definitely deserve that label. "Let's just call it love and be done with that."

"I agree." She ran her hand over my face in the picture. "You were watching dolphins playing not far from your deck. I recall that moment perfectly. That was early on for us. I had no idea how long we'd last, so I wanted to capture as many pictures of you as I could. I thought they might well be all I would have to remember you by."

I ran my hands over her hips to cover her tummy. "Now, you hold a part of me within you. Weird, huh?"

"I'll say." She turned the page and found a picture I'd taken of her. "And when did you swipe my camera, Galen?"

"You'll see. I did it kind of often." It wasn't nearly as good as the pictures she took, but I thought I had managed to capture how much I thought about her back then.

"I was watching television." She looked back at me. "You had to have just been watching me."

"Yes, you were much more entertaining than anything on television." I pulled her hair back over her shoulder, then kissed her there. "You still are."

Closing the album, she turned in my arms and kissed me. "I suppose we should change and go find them."

I knew she was right. My mother had to be wondering where we were. If we didn't go down soon, we'd have her beating at our bedroom door.

"I'm almost positive that on a sunny day like this, we'll find my parents lounging in the solarium." I pushed the French doors open, and there they were.

My father jumped up. "Well, what do we have here? A couple of newlyweds?"

"Not yet," I let them know.

My mother's frown could've made a clown cry. "No?" She came to us, taking Ariel's hands in hers. "I've missed you, Ariel."

"I've missed you, too." She kissed my mother on the cheek. "We're going to get married very soon. At Galen's resort, we're thinking. And all the children can be in the wedding, too."

"That would be nice." Ma looked at me. "How soon can we expect this to happen, son?"

I laughed. "Why, you in a rush for some grandkids or something, Ma?"

She shrugged. "What makes you think that?"

"Oh, maybe the sign above the bed," I said.

"And the bassinet filled with things for a newborn," Ariel added.

Ma blushed. "Was that going too far?"

Ariel shook her head. "No, I understand." Ariel looked at me and winked. "Galen has something to tell you both." She stepped back and put her arm around me. The jacket she'd put on hid her bulging belly. "I hope you won't be too disappointed. It's about children."

The shade of white my mother went kind of frightened me. "You don't want to have children yet, do you?" She threw her hands in the air. "Or ever, right? Oh, Galen, please. I know you're a busy man, but taking time for family is a must."

Before I could say anything, my father interjected. "Now, don't go making them feel as if they have to have children. It's okay if they don't want any. We've got plenty of grandkids already."

My mother wasn't happy with his idea. "But I want to see some kids with Galen's features. And Ariel and he would make gorgeous grandbabies for us. This is so disappointing. I'm sorry, I can't contain it. I'm a grandmother at heart—everyone who knows me knows that."

"Why don't you just focus on that wedding for now," my father replied, ever the peacemaker. "That'll be fun for you and take up about as much time as a grandbaby would. For a while anyway."

Ma still looked like she'd been served a mud pie, complete with worms. "Well, I suppose I could try to distract myself with that." She looked at Ariel. "If you're okay with my help."

"I would love it," Ariel gushed. "I've never planned or even thought about a wedding. Your help will be so valuable. And I've got another problem that I hope you can help me with. It's about the dress."

My mother shook her head. "Nothing to worry about there. My sister is an excellent seamstress. She made all of my daughters' wedding dresses. She can make yours too if you'd like."

"I'm glad to hear that." Ariel smiled at me. "I have no idea what size I'll be when the day finally comes. Knowing we'll have a seamstress right there to make alterations will be fantastic."

Ma looked a bit bewildered. "And why would ya have to be making alterations then, dear?"

I took over. "Well, we're not sure how quickly Ariel will be growing."

My father looked confused. "Growing?"

The urge to laugh nearly left me speechless, but I overcame it. "Yes, growing. You see, Ariel's and I will be having some twins in about five months. A boy and a girl. So you can see our problem, right?"

The looks on my parents' faces were priceless. And when Ariel pulled the camera out from under her jacket to snap those expressions, I knew we had another great one to add to the album.

We'd done it. We'd overcome everything to get to our happily ever after. And things had never looked brighter.

The End

If you want to read the entire Island of Love Series at a discount, you can get the complete box set by clicking here.

Bad Boy Billionaire Romance Series: Island of Love Box Set

https://books2read.com/u/3Lgklo